Scrambled

Lake Erie Mysteries, Volume 3

Olivia Breen

Published by Olivia Breen, 2021.

This is a work of fiction. Similarities to real people, places, or events are entirely coincidental.

SCRAMBLED

First edition. June 18, 2021.

ISBN: 979-8201515096

Written by Olivia Breen.

Chapter 1

Yaka Hula Hickey Dula.

I was standing at the bar on the deck of the *Angel's Trumpet*—a one-of-a-kind luxury pirate ship—about to order a cocktail. The sexy man behind the bar with the perfect five o'clock shadow and wavy dark hair looked me right in the eye and said it again. "Yaka Hula Hickey Dula."

I looked around and behind me, expecting to see whomever the bartender was talking to. There was no burly Hawaiian man, nor was there a clown. This left only me as the object of the strange greeting. I pride myself on being able to read people, but this guy had me stumped.

"Excuse me? I think you have me mixed up with someone else."

He flashed me a mischievous smile and held up a martini glass filled with a tropical-looking concoction. "Or are you in the mood for a Naked Lady?"

My mouth opened to speak, but nothing came out. If the guy wasn't drop-dead gorgeous, I would have slapped him by now. The look on my face must have told him what my voice was unable to convey.

"I'm sorry. I wasn't trying to be rude. Just having a little fun with these cocktail names. I'm Derek by the way. I assume congratulations are in order. You're obviously here because you're one of the recipe contest winners." He flashed his movie star smile at me again and handed me a laminated card with an extensive list of drinks featuring Paradise Rum. About halfway down the list, right below Daiquiri and Mojito, was, you guessed it, Yaka Hula Hickey Dula. According to the description it was a Hawaiian-style rum martini consisting of equal parts dark rum, dry vermouth, and pineapple juice. It sounded pretty good.

I shook my head and smiled. "Well, Derek, you had me going. I'm Francie, and yes, I'm a guest here for Pirate Fest. This ship is incredible, and I haven't even made it past the top deck yet. This is quite a spread the Paradise Rum people put out."

"They spared no expense for this weekend, and I was excited when I scored this bartending gig. I get to sample the winning recipes and meet the awesome people who created them. Not to mention, this ship is every guy's pirate fantasy come true." He grabbed a handful of nuts from the bowl on the bar and shook them like a pair of dice.

"So, Francie, what's your special talent?" He gave his fist one more shake before tossing his snack into his mouth.

I wasn't sure if he was flirting with me or simply enjoying his creative word play, but just in case, I decided to get back to the business of ordering a cocktail. I scanned the list of rum cocktails again, trying to choose one. "Seriously, what do you recommend?"

I should have seen it coming. "Why, the Naked Lady, of course."

Yikes. Was it just me, or was it getting hot around here?

I looked around for a distraction and was relieved to find my best friend June had caught up with me after making a quick detour to check into her hotel. She must have heard part of the conversation because she was chuckling as she helped herself to the drink list in my hand.

After a quick look at the selections, she handed the menu back to me, batted her long lashes at Derek and said, "Do you get bonus points for knowing the words to the Hawaiian song?"

I had no idea what she was talking about, but I knew whatever it was, it was going to be good.

June's sweet pixie face had the same effect on Derek it had on nearly every man who had the pleasure of making her acquaintance. He was doomed.

"There's no way you know the words to that song."

"Wanna bet? Al Jolson for sure. Some time between 1916 and 1920." She paused before delivering the final blow. "'Down Hawaii way, where I chanced to stray, / On an evening I heard a Hula maiden play'...should I go on?"

"Unbelievable! Are you a musician or something? I'm Derek, by the way."

"Nice to meet you. I'm June. Not a musician but a freelance journalist. I've got a lot of useful facts stored up for just such occasions."

Derek was intrigued. "Are you a food artist too?"

"No. I'm covering the pirate festivities for an article I'm writing. I'm staying at a hotel, but I'm standing in for Francie's husband until he can join her."

She didn't have to remind me I was a married woman—happily married at that. This was supposed to be a very special anniversary weekend for Hammond and me. I worked hard all summer perfecting my pirate stew and entering the Paradise Rum recipe contest, so when I was informed I was one of three winners, Hamm and I started planning our romantic, fun-filled getaway aboard the *Angel's Trumpet*.

At the last minute, Hamm was detained at our homeport, Beacon Pointe. An uneducated boater had pumped waste into the water causing all boat traffic in the marina to come to an immediate halt while the EPA was called in for an emergency cleanup. We couldn't take our boat across the lake to South Bass Island like we had planned, and Hamm was uncomfortable leaving until he was sure there would be no other fallout from the accident. He suggested he stay behind and join up with me later, so June and I took the ferry across the lake to Put-in-Bay, and now here I was being treated to free drinks at the Paradise Rum welcome reception with my best friend instead of my husband. I was ready for that cocktail.

"Make us a couple of those Hinky Doodles. After all the hype, I need to taste this thing."

No sooner had I placed our order, I had the drink menu snatched out of my hand yet again. There was a third woman at the bar now, and she apparently was in dire need of a drink.

"I'll take two Booty Drops. Make them virgin," the woman demanded. "And have someone bring them to me and my daughter. We'll be talking to the Paradise Rum promotions rep over by the hors d'oeuvres."

The woman's rudeness toward Derek startled and appalled me. To his credit, he took it all in stride. I guess bartenders get used to dealing with all sorts of personalities. That's probably why he flirted with the friendly ones. He gave her a little salute, turned his back, and got to the business of preparing her order.

Instead of leaving as promised, the annoying woman spoke again. "Mrs. Egg, is that you? I thought I recognized you."

Her voice was like fingernails dragging down a chalkboard. I had to count to ten and take a deep breath before giving her my full attention. It didn't take me long to put a name with the voice. Marla Fuller was the mother of one of my daughter Beth's college swim team teammates. It wasn't only her voice that made a lasting impression. Her haughty stature and jet-black hair streaked with a swath of white made me think of Cruella DeVil. The fact that her daughter, Liz, who stood beside and a little behind her, was wearing a black-and-white polka dot T-shirt cemented the image in my brain.

"Oh, hi, Mrs. Fuller," I said through clenched teeth and a pasted-on smile. It took all my powers of politeness not to remind her for the umpteenth time that my last name was Egge and rhymed with ledge, not leg. "Are you a guest of someone staying on the ship this weekend?"

"Oh heavens, no!" She fluttered her fake eyelashes at me to emphasize the ridiculousness of my comment. "I'm a special guest of Captain Cole Blackhart, the famous pirate. I won a recipe contest for my Triple-X Rum Cake. It's to die for! I was allowed to bring a guest along, so I invited my daughter, Elisabeth."

Then it clicked. Marla's daughter, Elisabeth, aka Liz, was the member of Beth's swim team who was banned from the annual end-of-year camping trip for doing something inappropriate after the last meet. That explained the sullen expression on the girl's face. I debated whether to one-up her by explaining that I too was a guest of Captain Blackhart, but my recipe won first prize and would be the main course of our dinner. In the end, I kept quiet, deciding it would be worth it to see the look on her face when she watched me receive the top honor.

"Two virgin Booty Drops m'lady. Or as I like to call them, grapefruit juice with a lime." Derek winked at me as he handed over the juice. I liked this guy, and decided I was going to leave him a generous tip. Mrs. Full of Herself snatched the drinks and mumbled something under her breath. She shoved a glass at her daughter and stomped across the deck to the hors d'oeuvres table and the rum rep who would surely be impressed by her choice of drinks.

Derek shook his head as he watched the pair retreat. "There's never a lack of entertainment with this job."

While Derek got to the task of putting together our Hawaiian martinis, June and I focused on giving our surroundings our full attention. We were standing in the middle of a magical ship like nothing I had ever seen or even imagined.

The repurposed pirate ship was anchored in the municipal marina in the heart of Put-in-Bay. It cast a massive shadow across the harbor stretching over a quarter of the docks. I couldn't believe the impressive vessel was to be my home for the next three days.

"I'm really sorry about the mess back at the marina, but it'll be fun to have a girl's night on board this beauty."

I had to agree. I looked forward to sharing some of my time here with June before Hamm arrived and she moved over to the Sparrow's Nest Inn where she had her reservation for the weekend. It was a quaint hotel right in the center of the main drag, adjacent to the popular Chicken Barbecue Patio. The rooms were clean and comfortable, even if you had to leave them to use the communal bath facility in the hall. From pirate ships to B&B's—it was all part of the island experience.

"Here you go, ladies." Derek handed each of us a frosty martini glass.

I was not disappointed. It tasted like happiness in a glass. "Great drink, Derek. And to think I would have probably ordered a strawberry daiquiri if you hadn't been so clever. Just one thing I need to know. What the heck does Yaka Hula Hickey Dula mean?"

Derek laughed. "I have no idea. I just like the way it sounds. June's the expert. Maybe she can enlighten us."

We both stared at her while she munched her pineapple garnish. "I hate to break the sad news, but it doesn't mean anything. When the song was written, Hawaiian music was all the rage and songwriters made up words and phrases that fit their mood and style."

"Huh." I speared my own pineapple. "Kind of like 'Do wah diddy diddy dum diddy do' in the sixties?"

"Exactly."

"I feel so much smarter now," Derek said. "Thanks for the music history lesson. I'm sure it'll come in handy. Enjoy your stay this weekend, and be sure to come back to try some more new rum drinks. I'm a graduate of the Paradise Rum Cocktail College and can make any drink you can think of and then some." He smiled and turned his attention to two new customers at the opposite end of the bar.

"Do you think that's a real college?" June asked.

"Looking the way that man looks, he can say whatever he wants. But seriously, he could be a biochemical engineer moonlighting in the off-season, for all we know. People are rarely just one thing."

"Agreed. And even when you think you know someone, he turns out to be a stranger."

Time to change the subject. June was recently divorced, and in spite of her friendly outgoing personality, there was a wounded spot in her heart.

"How about we find a seat over by the hors d'oeuvres and do some people-watching while we finish our drinks," I suggested.

Looking around at the polished wood deck, the gleaming brass fittings, and the twinkling white lights strung from the masts and riggings, I tried to imagine the way the *Angel's Trumpet* would have looked in 1813 when the Battle of Lake Erie had been fought.

First of all, she would have had a crew of about a hundred fifty men and boys who manned her sails, carronades, and long guns. This weekend, the crew would consist of only about twenty percent of the original number. Their duties, unlike the original crew, would center on catering to the wants and needs of six special guests, including myself, who had won their places aboard this battleship-turned-luxury liner by creating delicious recipes, the likes of which, I was sure, never passed the lips of the sailors aboard the warship two centuries ago.

Boys would be carrying trays of hors d'oeuvres and fancy drinks instead of black powder charges. There would be no firing of muskets atop the masts onto enemy ships. Orders from the captain would be to refill ice buckets and turn down high thread-count Egyptian cotton sheets in the cabins of the renovated interior of the ship that now slept thirty, not one hundred fifty.

We found two chairs as far away from the Fullers as we could manage. June set her drink down and pulled her camera out of her bag. She took her time framing her shot. "The light is perfect behind the sails. My editor is going to love this."

She took a few more photos before tucking her camera safely back into her bag and settling into her deck chair. From our vantage point, I could see the front of the ship and was mesmerized by the intricately carved mermaid at the bow emerging seamlessly from the polished teak hull. Angel wings on her back gave her a unique appearance unlike any depiction of a mermaid I had ever seen. Her arms were stretched back and out at her sides, as if bracing her body against the wind. In one hand she held a trumpet-shaped flower. Even her tail was distinctive. The traditional scales were arranged in a coil pattern giving it a serpentine look. The contrast of the wings and tail elicited complex images of the struggle between good and evil. Whoever the artist was had captured the essence of the *Angel's Trumpet* without using a single word.

"It's magnificent," I exclaimed. "I can just picture old Captain Blackhart shouting to his crew, ordering someone to walk the plank."

"Well, why are we sitting here gawking? Our drinks are gone and we've waited long enough. Let's go check out the interior."

"I'm ready." I looked at the empty martini glasses on the table. "But before we head down to the cabin, let's order one more of these. We can enjoy them while we settle into the room."

June needed no convincing. "That's an excellent plan. Wait here with the stuff. This round's on me."

While June skipped off toward the bar, two fingers raised in greeting, I readjusted the shoulder strap of my oversized purse, debating whether or not I should reposition it across my body instead of wearing it on my shoulder which would have made juggling my drink, room key and bag of goodies I had received upon registration a lot more manageable. Before I could convince myself to make the adjustment, June was back with the drinks. Oh well. Soon I'd be able to dump the whole load in our cabin and jump for joy or, more likely, put my feet up and savor my second tropical drink while plotting the best way to squeeze in as much fun as possible with my best friend before Hamm joined me and she moved out to complete her assignment.

June was in front of me, heading aft along the gunnel, caressing the gleaming teak rail as she went. I adjusted my purse strap once again and caught up to her. When we made it to the back of the ship, we stopped to take in the breathtaking vista of the lake. The Caribbean music from the band near the bar was faint here. My mind wandered off, imagining this same view some two hundred years ago. The lake breeze ruffled my hair, and I took in a big breath, feeling both grounded to the past and exhilarated for what the future had in store.

"Oh, June, don't you wish this moment could last forever?"

"It is beautiful, isn't it? I'm guessing you'd prefer your everlasting moment to be in the company of your ever-loving husband instead of me though." She brushed a strand of spiky blond hair off her forehead.

I thought of Hamm again. He was going to love getting up close and personal with those planks, as well as the pilot station, the decks, rails, sails, and every other detail right down to the glue and screws holding the whole vessel together. His love of all things nautical was real and contagious.

"Oh, yes, but you know what I meant." I didn't get a chance to say more.

Bam! I was whacked on the side of the head by something flapping and swirling like a rogue rainbow.

"What the heck?" I screamed and swatted at my attacker. My newly acquired cocktail was reduced to a pretty pink puddle at my feet. The stem of the plastic martini glass pointed accusingly up at me. Furious now, I slipped my designer leather handbag off my shoulder, took aim, and flung it toward the thing, but it hit nothing. The offending projectile—more specifically, the parrot—had moved on, screeching something that sounded like "Hang on tight. Hang on tight," and my purse rocketed into the empty space it left behind, gathering momentum as it flew over the deck rail and splashed unceremoniously into the lake.

I saw my life flash before my eyes as the contents of my beautiful leather satchel popped out of their cozy jumble and made ready to sink or swim. In all my years, my purse has been my constant companion, always there when I needed something in a pinch, from an EpiPen to a phone charger. Now the bag and all its lovely inhabitants were sinking down to Davy Jones's locker to rest among the other lost treasures at the bottom of the lake.

There was no way I was going to take this lying down. I had the feeling I was being mocked or challenged as I raced back and forth the length of the deck searching for the fiendish fowl so I could ring its scrawny rainbow neck. Frustrated by my failure, I leaned over the rail so far June had to grab me around my knees before I vaulted myself over the side of the ship. She hauled me back from the brink and plopped onto the deck beside me, holding my shoulders as I sobbed into her shirt.

"Come on, Francie." After giving me what she thought was the appropriate time to mourn my loss, June took my elbow and helped me up to a standing position. "Let's go find your room. Everything will be okay. After all, it's not as if someone died. A purse and its contents can be replaced."

I glared at her. I knew I was being irrational, but I couldn't help it. In my mind, I felt like someone *had* died. She got the hint.

Swallowing the lump in my throat, I followed her to the middle of the deck where the door leading into the living quarters of the ship was located. We made our way down a short set of steps into a narrow corridor and followed the instructions printed on placards decorated with various pirate-themed illustrations until we arrived at my designated stateroom. June opened the cabin door and stepped aside to let me enter first. Once inside, I smiled in spite of myself. In front of me stood a bed that looked like a wedding dress, all white and poofy. In the middle of the bedspread was a single long-stemmed red rose and a distinctive Blue Box with a white bow.

"Oh, it couldn't be!" I squealed, bending to take the box and bring it close to my face for inspection. The memory of my drowned handbag was fading fast. Boy, am I fickle.

I gave the bow a tug and peeked under the lid. It dawned on me Hamm had managed to coerce someone with access to our cabin into making sure his surprise gifts were in place when we arrived. What he hadn't managed and couldn't have foreseen, was that he wouldn't be there to see the look on my face when I opened my gift. A twinge of sadness touched my heart, but it was replaced by a sense of teenage infatuation when I saw what was in the box.

I held up a delicate gold chain with a captain's wheel pendant dangling from it. The eight spokes of the wheel were gold. The outer circle sparkled with diamonds, and in the center of the wheel was an exquisite solitaire. I turned it over and squinted to read the tiny letters etched around the wheel. "Don't give up the ship."

To the casual visitor to Put-in-Bay, the phrase was a fun saying that could be spotted all over the island—white letters emblazoned on marine blue—on T-shirts, flags, souvenirs and signs.

"I don't get it," June said looking puzzled as she read the inscription over my shoulder. "I didn't realize Hamm was such a history buff. Does he really think you would find a battle cry romantic?"

"Of course he would. And it is! Sit down and let me tell you a little story."

June sat down on the edge of the bed and folded her hands demurely in her lap like a schoolgirl waiting for enlightenment. "I'm all ears professor."

I sat in the accent chair facing her and began. "On the morning of September 10, 1813, Master Commandant Oliver Hazard Perry made preparations to sail forth to engage the British right here in these waters. Just before the skirmish began, Perry called out to his men, 'We have met the enemy and they are ours!' Then he hoisted his battle flag, inscribed 'Don't Give Up the Ship,' and calling out the same to his crew, the Battle of Lake Erie began."

"Wow, Francie, that was a speech fit for center stage. How long have you been waiting to give that performance? And more to the point, what does it have to do with a beautiful necklace from a world famous jeweler?"

"Don't you see June? Commodore Perry's battle was nothing compared to the everyday battles Hamm and I faced early on in our marriage. Raising twins as a stay-at-home mom with a husband who spent sixty plus hours a week at his firm trying to impress the partners was a real war for sanity. One day, I called Hamm at work and threatened to run away to a deserted island. He was engrossed in something and tried to calm me down by saying, "Don't give up the ship, Hon." For all I know, he read it off a notepad from PIB or saw it on a pen someone had left at the office, but it made me laugh at the time, and the saying stuck. Any time things get rough, we remind each other to not give up the ship."

"Well, that makes sense now. And I have to admit, it's original and it suits you." She stuck out her hand. "Give it here. Turn around and let me help you put it on."

I did as instructed, and June fastened the clasp behind my neck.

"Well, I'm impressed," June whispered, letting a slow whistle pass her lips when I turned around. "You've got yourself a keeper."

"I do, don't I? I don't take him for granted either. I know I'm a very lucky girl." Girl might have been pushing my luck. I had seen forty come and go, but woman sounded old.

"I think I'll go freshen up and let you enjoy your moment." June stepped into the bathroom, giving me a little space to soak up all the details of Hamm's sweet gesture. Not only was I blessed with the best husband, but I also have the best friend anyone could ask for.

My immediate thought was to call Hamm and thank him for the wonderful surprise. I had no pockets in the sundress I was wearing, so guess where I'd stashed my phone? The ugly truth hit me hard, but I wasn't going to let it ruin my husband's perfect gift. I was about to call out to June and ask to borrow her phone when I noticed an old-fashioned rotary phone on the nightstand. It was real and it was functional. It had been a long time since I saw a landline at a dock, but before the dawn of ubiquitous cell service, it was standard operating procedure for marinas to offer phone service to patrons. I was thankful the sponsors decided to keep the decor low tech.

When June came back into the room, I was smiling and fingering my new necklace. She looked around the room and back to me. "Who were you talking to? Was someone here?"

"No," I answered dreamily. "I was talking to Hamm. He asked me to call him when we got here, and now I know why. He wanted to make sure I got his gift. I got sidetracked and didn't remember to tell him about that crazy parrot knocking my purse overboard."

"I don't want to hear what you were discussing. Let's get ready to meet your shipmates and this pirate captain people keep talking about." She stopped and gave me a long hard look. "You need to pour yourself a tall glass of ice water. Your cheeks are flushed."

Chapter 2

I got down to the business of unpacking, and June dumped the contents of her overnight bag on the bed. "What's the dress code for the reception dinner, Francie? I packed for a weekend of pirate parties, relaxing, and writing, not hobnobbing with famous chefs and business moguls."

"You can't go wrong with something classic," I answered, but when I looked over the array of wardrobe choices flung across the bed, I bit my tongue. This was going to be interesting—fun but interesting.

June was holding up a hot pink lamé top with sequined spaghetti straps. There was a black leather mini skirt and sky-high heels set apart from the rest of the jumble. "You aren't wearing that are you?"

"I'm considering it, why? I look amazing in this outfit. Worried I might steal your thunder?"

"Haha! No, of course not. I've seen you in that outfit, and you would definitely turn heads, but I'm thinking something a little more traditional is in order."

"Well, I hadn't exactly planned to attend a dinner party this weekend. I wouldn't even be here if Hamm hadn't decided to stay behind to make sure our boats were okay after the EPA was finished cleaning up at the marina. I can't believe some guy was dumb enough to pump gas into his waste tank and then let the whole foul mess spill over into the water. Jeez. Not only is the water contaminated with you-know-what, but a tiny spark or a cigarette tossed in the lake could cause the place to go up in flames."

"I know he did the right thing, but I feel like I abandoned him. I offered to stay behind with him, but he insisted I come." I shoved the jumble of clothes onto the floor, flopped down on the bed and sighed.

June plopped down next to me and reached over to touch my new necklace. Flipping over the pendant, she said, "Hamm didn't give up his ship, Francie. You know he wouldn't have been able to relax until he knew for sure that everything was taken care of at the marina. It was sweet of him to offer to check up on my houseboat as well. He didn't want you to give up any part of this trip. You earned it, so let's stop pouting and start sharing clothes so I don't show up looking like the entertainment and embarrass you."

I couldn't help but smile. "Thank goodness you're open to suggestions. I don't have a spare dinner outfit, but I have an idea that might work." I hopped off the bed and held out my hand. "Give me that top you're holding and go put this on instead." I handed her my brightly-flowered, one-piece swimsuit."

"Uh, Okay."

June looked at me like my mind had flown over the side of the ship with my purse, but she didn't argue. Minutes later, she emerged from the bathroom wearing the Hawaiian tank suit I had offered her and looking skeptical. The top of the suit was filled out nicely, but the bottom half sagged on her.

The stretchy fabric accommodated my figure, but her hips were three sizes smaller than mine, and she reminded me of my daughter Beth playing dress-up in my closet when she was eight. While she was changing, I had put on her shiny pink top and paired it with a lightweight pinstriped blazer, slim black capris, and strappy black leather sandals.

"Wow! You sure classed that shirt up, and standing next to me in this ridiculous swimsuit, you're sure to be the belle of the ball."

"Don't worry. This is going to work; trust me."

I tossed her my high-waisted, wide-leg palazzo pants and a sheer, red crop-top I used as a beach cover-up. Obediently, she pulled on the pants, which immediately drooped, to her hips. Before she had time to complain, I handed her my wide, black belt. Luckily, it was elastic. She added it to her ensemble, and it did the trick. We were making progress. Next, she shrugged into the top and tied the sheer fabric at her waist. I stood back and admired my handiwork.

It was time for June to add her own flair. She stepped into a pair of high-top yellow Converse sneakers. The long flowy pants brushed the floor, and her shoes weren't visible, but I knew when she walked or sat down and crossed her legs, the footwear would peek out and add just the right pizzazz.

After adding our finishing touches, we stood in front of the full-length mirror attached to the bathroom door and took in our reflection. I decided to let my brown curls hang loose around my shoulders rather than submitting them to the will of my flat iron. I added a pair of gold hoop earrings to complement my new necklace, and topped off my look with a hot pink lipstick to pull everything together. June went with a fresh look of sheer lip-gloss and minimal jewelry, but true to form, she now sported a funky red streak in her short spiky hair. It coordinated perfectly with her new outfit.

"I think we pulled it off," June announced. "I guess I should've trusted you."

"Yep. Being in theater does have its advantages," I agreed.

I was proud of the way both our looks turned out. After spending fifteen years in the drama department at the local college, I'd mastered the art of costuming. Putting together original fashion looks with whatever clothes and accessories were at my disposal came naturally to me. Working with our personal belongings made it a piece of cake.

We congratulated ourselves on our success with a toast, sharing the last of June's martini since mine hadn't made it back to the room. "Here's to an unforgettable weekend," June raised the glass, took a sip, and handed it to me.

"I second that," I said, finishing the cocktail. "Let's go see what this pirate dinner is all about."

I felt naked without my purse as I handed my key card to June since I had no place to stash it. On the bright side, I now had the perfect reason to shop, and when Hamm got here, I'd have access to cash. The island boutiques were full of one-of-a-kind accessories, and no one could begrudge me the purchase of a replacement handbag and maybe a matching wallet.

We retraced our steps, following the directional placards to our destination. We'd have found the dining room without them. An inviting Caribbean melody wafted into the hall along with the sweet scent of coconut. Right outside the entrance stood a six-foot carved and painted pirate with one hand on a scabbard at his side and a mug bearing the Paradise Rum logo in his other hand. I was about to put my arm around the statue and ask June to snap a souvenir photo, when I changed course and rushed past the pirate and through the door.

"What was that all about?" June asked as she scurried to my side.

"Did you see the parrot on his shoulder? I don't know if I'll ever be able to look at one of those creatures again after being assaulted."

June shook her head, humoring me as we made our way to the last two open seats at the round table in the ship's intimate dining room. It looked more like it belonged in a five-star hotel than a renovated battleship. The mahogany walls and plank floors glowed with a patina from decades of meticulous polishing. Soft light emanated from brass sconces evenly spaced throughout the room. Beautiful blue hydrangeas at the table's center complemented the blue and yellow china and soft yellow linens. Each of the six place settings included enough flatware for a royal banquet. I might be intimidated by blustering birds, but I wasn't worried about misusing utensils. I had mastered the art of proper dining back when I was interviewing for the position of head of CSU's drama department. You never know when you might be called upon to demonstrate the proper use of a salad fork.

I shook out my napkin, smoothed it on my lap, and folded my hands like I was born for this role. The look on Marla Fuller's face was priceless, making me forget all about my encounter with the painted parrot. Her mouth was open but nothing came out which I took as an added bonus. Marla's daughter Liz looked exactly as she had earlier—sullen and supremely uninterested in her mother, me, or any of her tablemates. Two young men sat to the right of June. They had to be the third contest winner and his guest. I introduced myself and was pleased no one questioned me when I introduced June as my dinner partner. There were a few laughs and expressions of concern when I relayed Hamm's predicament and the reason for the last-minute change. I assured everyone, myself most of all, they'd meet my husband tomorrow. Marla recovered from her initial shock, made a respectable comeback and joined in the banter. She managed to avoid eye contact with me, and tried unsuccessfully to draw her daughter into the conversation.

Captain Blackhart entered the dining room from an unobtrusive door near the bar across from the main entrance, and the table went silent. We were finally face-to-face with the man we had heard about, imagined, and discussed. He lived up to every one of my personal fantasies. He was tall and tan. His kohl-rimmed eyes were the color of topaz. Lush black hair cascaded around his shoulders. A few strands around his face were braided and embellished with beads. For a second, I wondered if it would be rude to ask him what hair products he used, but lucky for me, I wasn't given the time to act on my thought and embarrass myself. He picked up a crystal goblet from the tray of a passing server and raised his hand in a toast revealing an assortment of silver, leather, and beaded bracelets under the snow-white ruffle of his cuff.

"Good evening. As you all have likely figured out, I am your host for the weekend, Captain Cole Blackhart. It is my pleasure to welcome and congratulate three special people this evening. Francesca, Marla, and Zach, you have earned the top

honors of the prestigious Paradise Rum recipe competition."
He nodded his head as he spoke each of our names. "I hope
you're finding your way around the *Angel's Trumpet* and
discovering her many charms. I'll save the speech-making for
another time and allow you to enjoy your meal and one
another's company. Here's to a weekend you'll talk about for
years to come. Enjoy!"

Short and sweet. I liked that. Cheers were shared all
around the table. I clinked my own crystal goblet containing
the smoothest spiced rum I'd ever tasted, first to June's glass
and then to Marla Fuller's, probably a bit harder than was
called for. I wasn't thrilled about sitting in such close proximity
to the irritating woman and her whiny daughter. It was worth
it though, when she was finally obliged to speak directly to me,
and I smiled sweetly as she sputtered her lame congratulations
for my winning the main course recipe category. Okay, maybe
my smile was a bit more smug than sweet, but hey, I was polite.

I was more interested in getting to know the other two
people at our table. Zach and Bradley were seated next to June,
which put them across from me at the round table. They were
an intriguing pair. According to the bio flyer handed to me as
I took my seat, they were twin brothers. They looked nothing
alike, but it was safe to assume they shared some of the same
interests since they were here together. Being the mother of
twins, I'm always interested in hearing about the dynamics
between other sets of twins.

It was Zach's recipe for jerk wings with rum butter glaze
that had secured him and his brother a spot at the winner's
table. He was of average height and weight. His round,
wire-frame glasses added an air of intelligence to his friendly

face. There was no hair on his head, but his short goatee and scruffy sideburns were noticeably red. It was probably a good thing there was no official dress code included in our welcome packets because I had a feeling his long-sleeved, band logo T-shirt, khaki shorts, and flip flops were his everyday uniform, and he didn't feel obligated to veer from it even for a celebration where he was one of the guests of honor. Fine by me. I liked people with strong self-identities.

I couldn't wait to sample the appetizers and vowed not to eat too many, since as much as I hated to admit it, I needed to save room for Marla's rum cake. As we savored Zach's delicious wings, unashamedly licking our fingers between bites, Bradley entertained us with stories from his brother's doctoral research about the real-life pirates who had sailed among the Lake Erie islands two centuries ago. Bradley was yin to Zach's yang. He seemed content to be along for the ride. Tall and lanky, he had spiky brown hair and a clean-shaven face. His nose, chin, and cheekbones were all sharp angles. A pale blue bowling shirt allowed his colorful sleeve of tattoos to capture my attention and stir my curiosity as he heartily drank from his crystal goblet of spiced rum and regaled us with his engaging tales. I thought maybe Zach had chosen his brother to accompany him because of his gregarious nature and social skills. Bradley's outgoing personality rounded out Zach's creative genius in the quieter fields of cooking and academic research.

As we progressed through the meal, Marla kept prodding her daughter and encouraging her to eat more, while Liz, still wearing the black-and-white polka-dot top from earlier, looked like she was auditioning to play the least interested person on the planet. She had the role in the bag, no question. June was multitasking—batting her lovely long eyelashes at Bradley while consuming mass quantities of food. She made it work. I split my energy between filling my mental notebook with details to share with Hamm and filling my belly with a hearty portion of the main course—my original pirate stew prepared to perfection by the ship's own professional chef.

Speaking of professional chefs, when Chef Truffle came through the door, all activity ceased for the second time. His physical appearance was as far from my mental image of a ship's cook as was possible. He must have been close to seven feet tall. I wondered if he was an NFL linebacker in his spare time and thought it might be hard to tell him and his industrial refrigerator apart from a distance. He stretched his arms toward the room, revealing intricate tattoos depicting a pirate's life in living color. Bradley's eyes grew wide with appreciation for their mutual passion for body art.

"Welcome, friends, and congratulations winners!" Truffle proclaimed in a booming voice.

"Welcome friends. Welcome friends," cawed the multicolored creature perched on his shoulder." My eyes grew wide, and I balled my hands into fists under the table. Unbelievable. I'd recognize that offensive fowl anywhere.

"We had over three hundred entries in our Paradise Rum recipe contest, so the three of you should be thrilled and proud to have been chosen as the winners. As you know, I have prepared each of your recipes for you to share with your guests in the winner's circle tonight."

"Winner, winner, what's for dinner?" Now my teeth were clenched, and I felt the muscles between my shoulder blades tightening.

"Isn't my Pretty Boy clever?" Chef Truffle stroked the bird's feathers as he continued his opening remarks. "You'll all have many opportunities to get to know him during your time aboard the *Angel's Trumpet*. He has free reign of the ship and is friendly and inquisitive."

"Let's be friends. Let's be friends," the bird squawked, spreading his wings and striking a pose before rising from Truffle's shoulder and taking flight. He circled the room once and then a second time, swooping too close to my head for my liking on his third pass. With great effort, I swallowed the scream threatening to escape my throat. Only after Pretty Boy departed through the open doorway could I safely take in air again. I didn't trust myself to share my tale of woe with my dinner partners without getting emotional, so I kept my aversion to myself.

Without missing a beat, Truffle continued his speech. "There will be samplings of your dishes throughout the village restaurants and bars all weekend. I understand you will be attending several meet-and-greets during your time here, and I assure you the locals will be delighted to chat with you about your winning recipes, especially since all the events will feature free samples of Paradise Rum." Liz Fuller perked up at that announcement. "And finally, the good people in charge of this contest have prepared recipe cards complete with pictures, so you can distribute them as you wish."

Right on cue, a smiling pirate wench with bouncy red curls appeared at our table and handed each winner a stack of three-by-five, color-printed recipe cards. Chef Truffle wasn't kidding when he mentioned pictures. Right beside the full-color picture of my pirate stew was a not-too-shabby photo of yours truly. The ingredients and directions were printed neatly on the backside. I was impressed. It seemed these folks had thought of everything.

After giving us a few minutes to admire ourselves and trade recipe cards, Captain Blackhart came back on the scene, clearing his throat to bring us all back to order. "And now, while you enjoy your prize-winning dessert, I invite Mr. Parker Thorn, the Paradise Rum representative, to tell you more about the exciting things in store for you this weekend including a treasure hunt that will take you to some of the most popular sites on the island and a few lesser known ones guaranteed to serve up some surprises. It's been designed to entertain and enlighten you while engaging you in some friendly competition. Remember, Paradise Rum is still looking for its new spokesperson, and it could be you."

Mr. Thorn took it from there. "You'll be working in pairs—winners plus invited guests—to figure out clues leading you to the various locations where you will collect tokens and opportunities to earn extra points. The person with the highest score at the conclusion of the weekend will be named the next national spokesperson for Paradise Rum." He paused for dramatic effect and added, "After the required FBI background check of course." I caught his playful wink, but noticed Zach pulling at his collar and Marla shooting daggers at her daughter with her eyes. I had no worries. As a public employee, my fingerprints and background check were updated regularly courtesy of the university.

Thorn continued. "You'll appear in ads in newspapers and magazines as well as on TV and radio. There will be live appearances across the country too—all expenses paid, of course. Be thinking of a name for your team while you finish up your meals, and if you need anything at all, please don't hesitate to ask."

Marla's hand shot up, nearly knocking the fork out of my hand. Bradley leaned in close to June and whispered loud enough for me to hear. "I don't think he meant right this second, do you?" He rolled his eyes toward Marla, and June stifled a giggle behind her hand.

Parker Thorn was at our table in two long strides. He reached across me, taking Marla's hands, and pulling her to feet. "Marla, my dear, there's no need for such formality. Please, speak freely." He twirled her in a circle, expertly leading her away from the table and onto the makeshift dance floor between our table and the door Blackhart and Truffle had used earlier. It was the second time all night Liz looked remotely less than bored. The steel drum and ukulele players who had quit playing during dinner struck up a sunny tune, and before I knew it, Blackhart and Truffle were heading our way.

"Now we're cooking!" I exclaimed, getting into the festive mood. After all the food I just consumed, I welcomed a chance to dance off a few calories.

Captain Blackhart bowed ceremoniously and extended his hand toward me. "May I have the honor of this dance, Francesca?"

He helped me to my feet, and I followed him to the dance floor. Liz Fuller accepted Chef Truffle's invitation, and I smiled at the picture they created. I guessed Liz to be about five foot one. Truffle looked like he was swinging a rag doll, yet somehow, it was a gentle, almost poignant sight. I had to crane my neck over Blackhart's shoulder to find out whom June would end up with as a dance partner. Zach was inspecting his cuticles. Bradley was looking uncertain. I lost my line of sight for a minute while I was twirled and dipped by the charismatic pirate. When I next saw June, she was laughing in Bradley's arms. Zach had made his way to the bar and was deep in conversation with Derek, the bartender.

I let myself be swept up in the moment, swaying to the intoxicating island melodies and imagining myself on a tropical island dancing with a famous treasure hunter who only had eyes for me. This was easy. Ever since I'd started working on creating the perfect recipe featuring rum as an ingredient, I had become infatuated with the romantic history of lost treasure and those who searched for it. One story in particular had captured my imagination. It centered around a girl named Rose and her determination to keep her family's legacy out of the hands of marauding pirates. I often found myself sidetracked from my cooking experiments, delving deeper and deeper into the details of Rose's tale. I caught myself waking from dreams in which I had become the girl. Other times I was her friend, and once I was one of the pirates trying to trick her out of her heritage.

Pop! Uh oh. I should have been daydreaming and shimmying less and paying more attention to the tenuous nature of my wardrobe. June's lamé top had plenty of stretch, but the straps were no match for my gyrating shoulders. As soon as I jerked my hand up to grab the sparkly string of runaway rhinestones, I felt the second strap let loose. This was not going to end well, and I'd be adding one more item to my shopping list. Good thing I was still wearing my blazer.

"Excuse me, Captain," I whispered, reluctant to end my pirate frolic fantasy, but painfully aware of the urgency of my situation. "I need to visit the ladies' room." I left him standing alone in the middle of the floor while I rushed out of the room clutching the front of my top, and losing the battle. It sank lower and lower with each step I took. I was so intent on keeping my private parts private that I didn't see Liz and Chef Truffle standing in the hall until I nearly ran into them. I offered up an apology, but they never broke eye contact. I'm pretty sure they didn't even notice me.

I sighed in relief when the bathroom door closed behind me, but my relief was short-lived when I realized I didn't have a safety pin or even a paper clip to remedy my wardrobe malfunction. Nor did I have any way to let June know what had happened. I wasn't about to spend the rest of the evening hiding out in a powder room. Time to put my emergency fashion skills to the test. First, I wriggled out of the top and looked at the pathetic, stretched out piece of cloth in my hands. It was the opposite of sexy. Next, I worked on fastening the gold buttons on my blazer, pushing the sleeves up to my elbows, and assessing whether I could pull off wearing it on its own. After a few rounds of tucking and tugging, I was finally satisfied with the result and was about to take my chances back at the dinner party, when June bounced through the door, stopped at the sink, and splashed water on her face and neck.

"There you are, Francie. Is everything okay?" June patted her face with a paper towel. "I didn't see you slip away. Captain Blackhart cut in on Bradley and me, and he said you left kind of unexpectedly. He asked me to come check on you." She tilted her head and squinted at me.

I thought about hiding the ravaged pink top behind my back but realized the attempt at a cover-up would be laughable. I offered it up to my friend in lieu of an explanation. She took one look at the pathetic piece and tossed it in the trash. "I was bored with that thing anyway. Besides, you look sexy hot without it."

I re-evaluated my reflection and decided to believe her. Best friends don't lie to one another. "So, what did I miss? Did you see Liz and the chef in the hall? I nearly collided with them, and neither of them so much as blinked."

"Liz is back at the table with her mother. I think they're both pouting. When I left Blackhart to come find you, Marla asked him to dance. He gave her the cold shoulder and stalked out with Thorn right behind him. Chef Truffle never came back. Zach left for a while. He didn't seem interested in dancing, but he was back by the time I left."

"I think I'm ready to go back. I don't want to be rude, and if I limit myself to sitting, I think my outfit revisions will hold up."

When we got back to the dining room, I made a quick decision. "I'll meet you at the table. I'm going to get us an after dinner drink to go with what's left of my dessert."

June gave me a thumbs-up and headed right toward the table while I veered left to the bar.

"Hi, Derek. What kind of after dinner drink can you whip up for June and me? I'm doing research. If I'm going to be the next spokesperson for Paradise Rum, I should broaden my horizons, don't you think?"

Derek didn't answer. He wasn't even looking at me. His eyes were laser-focused on my cleavage. I cleared my throat and turned slightly.

"Uh. Um. Uh. Sorry. That's a beautiful...necklace you're wearing. The diamonds are practically blinding me." He grinned sheepishly.

"Nice save, bar boy. So, about those drinks."

"I guess I had that coming." He was trying so hard to maintain eye contact, I almost felt sorry for him. "Oh yeah. What was it you wanted, again?"

"Something to go with dessert, and you better not recommend a Naked Lady, or I might have to unleash my ninja moves on you."

"I hear you, Francie. How about a couple of Cocoa Locos? They can actually replace dessert. They're pretty rich, but what the heck. This is the time to splurge, right?"

"Sounds delicious, but it also sounds like there's chocolate in them, and June is allergic. What else have you got?"

"I can make you a Pyrat Passion instead. It's made with peach puree. Or maybe a Hot Caramel Buttered Rum."

"Decisions, decisions. I'll take one each of the last two. We can share."

While Derek prepared the drinks, I took a closer look at the room. In the dim light, the door by the bar was virtually undetectable. "Where does that door lead?" I asked Derek's back.

He gave a dismissive wave with his hand. "That's just the service entrance. It leads to the storage room and then back to the galley. You can't have cooks and servers running down the hall and in and out of the main entrance. With all the people who've been back and forth through that thing tonight, it would have put a real damper on the festivities."

"I hadn't thought of that. It makes sense."

"Why don't you go sit down? I'll bring these over. I wouldn't want you to spill them." He was staring at my chest again.

When I got back to the table, the whole gang was reassembled, and best of all, the plates hadn't been cleared. I had to hand it to Marla Fuller—her Triple X Rum Cake had earned its top honors, and I planned to show my approval by making sure no crumb was left behind.

We sipped our drinks, finished our food, and relived the highlights of the party. I left out the part about how I lost my shirt, but by the looks I was getting, I figured there was more than one version of the story being played out in the minds of my companions.

Finally, the conversation waned, and I could eat or drink no more. The Fuller ladies took their leave, and the twin brothers followed soon after.

June set her glass down and focused her attention on me. "What is it, Francie? You look like you have something on your mind."

"I was just thinking. Why don't we visit the galley before we turn in and ask the chef if he could box up some leftovers for Hamm. I know he'd enjoy everything on the menu tonight." I caught myself rubbing my pendant between my thumb and forefinger. "He's probably having popcorn and beer for dinner."

June smiled at me. "Sure, what can it hurt?"

Little did either of us know.

Chapter 3

The galley was located near the middle of the ship, making it necessary for all occupants, crew members and guests alike, to walk by it on their way to and from most locations. The heavy wooden door with a painted inlay of a bright-winged parrot (I shuddered at the sight) was not locked. June knocked then pushed the door inward and held it while I passed in front of her into the cool interior. Stainless steel surfaces gleamed all around me. For a pirate lair, the place sure was clean. Once again, I had to remind myself that the man who reigned over the space was a top-notch master chef, not a scurvy scalawag slinging slop for a ragtag crew.

My eyes fixed upon a glass-front refrigerator holding a bountiful assortment of sweet delicacies, so when my foot hit a soft lump of something on the floor, I tried to kick it aside and move on without taking my eyes off the beautiful still life in front of me. Whatever the obstruction was, it didn't budge, and I ended up tripping, stopping myself from toppling by smacking both palms down hard on the shining countertop. My first thought was of the fingerprints I was certain to leave on the pristine counter. I didn't want to answer to the chef for contaminating his workspace.

June was just entering the room. She flicked on the lights, transforming the entire space from a soft gleam into a dazzling expanse of reflective surfaces. "Hello? Anyone here? Where did you go, Francie?"

"Over here, by the fridge." I had regained my balance and looked down, curious to see what had impeded my progress. That's when I screamed. And screamed. I wrenched myself from the gruesome scene at my feet and flung myself sideways, almost into my friend's arms. I didn't have to explain the cause of my hysteria.

There, dressed in his white topcoat, his starched white toque crumpled beneath his head, lay the bulky form of the chef. The only things marring his uniform were the glinting silver handle of the expensive butcher's knife embedded in his chest and the dark red stain emanating from the point of impact.

June sprang into action. I, on the other hand, slumped slowly to the floor, clutching my knees and concentrating on not throwing up the remains of the meal the man lying motionless on the floor had so recently prepared for us.

"Don't touch anything, Francie. Take some deep breaths and stay put. I'm calling the police right now."

She needn't have worried. I wasn't moving. "Who would want to kill the chef? There's so much blood. I've never seen so much blood."

When June spoke next, it wasn't to me. "Yes, we're still here. We haven't notified the captain yet, or anyone else for that matter."

I wished I could hear the other side of the conversation. I was slowly regaining my composure, or at least I wasn't going to vomit or pass out.

June pressed the button on her phone to end the call and walked over to the door, opening it a crack and peering into the hall. All was calm. The evening was progressing according to plan for most of the people on the ship. I couldn't say the same for our own.

"What did the police say, June?"

"I asked to speak with Jack, but then I remembered he was out of town. He's testifying in Chicago."

Jack was Detective Jack Morgan. His jurisdiction included the Lake Erie islands and certain cities on the mainland. We met him last May when our paths crossed on Kelleys Island, where he was instrumental in saving our lives and putting a ruthless killer with ties to Chicago mobsters behind bars. Since then he and June had struck up the beginnings of a cautious romance. Hamm and I heartily approved of the pair, if indeed that's what they were.

"They said what you'd expect. Stay calm. Don't touch anything. Try to remember if you saw anything or anyone unusual this evening, especially right before we entered the galley."

"You mean like Liz and Truffle having a private conversation in the hall when they both should have been with us in the dining room?"

"Yeah, like that. I can't think of anything else. Can you?"

I could not. But then the sight of the service door flashed into my mind. "Do you think one of us should go look for Liz?

She must know something. I bet she was the last person to see Chef Truffle alive. You don't think she killed him, do you?"

June shook her head. "The detective told us to stay put. Besides, which one of us is going to volunteer to wait for him here?"

"Maybe someone was waiting for Truffle. There's a service door that leads from here to the storage room and then back to the dining room. Anyone could have come in and out without being seen, and according to Derek, there was a steady flow of people going in and out all evening." I slapped my hand over my mouth, and my eyes widened in a new realization. "Maybe the killer is still here," I whispered.

"I'm pretty sure we'd have seen him by now if he were. There's no place to hide and the lights are super bright."

"There's probably room for a person inside that fridge," I said.

"Let's focus on remembering everything we can. Besides, the refrigerator has a glass front. Even if someone was dumb enough to hide in there, we'd be able to see him without opening the door. Try to stay calm. The cops will be here any minute."

She said that last sentence in a loud, clear voice. Just in case.

Five minutes passed, then ten. The minutes felt like hours. I wanted so badly to do something—to open cupboards and drawers, to look under and behind things—but since we had strict instructions from the authorities not to disturb anything in this shiny crime scene, I had no choice but to stay put. Detective Morgan would be proud. June and I had a tendency to get ourselves mixed up in island crime investigations. We didn't do it on purpose, but this was the third time this year, trouble had knocked on our door, or rather had barged in uninvited.

I picked a spot in the corner farthest away from the recently departed Chef Truffle and sat on the floor. I missed my handbag. I couldn't take any surreptitious pictures with my phone or jot down notes or impressions about the details of my surroundings—details that seemed insignificant now but might prove crucial later on. I resigned myself to harnessing all my powers of observation and systematically committing everything to memory.

Finally, the door swung open. The man who entered didn't look like any law enforcement person I knew. His handsome, serious face had the look of someone who'd seen his share of rough times. The rest of him almost made me forget why we were gathered in the ship's galley after hours.

The detective stopped just inside the door, pulled a pair of blue latex gloves from the pocket of his blazer, and snapped them on. Following on his heels was a thin young man wearing thick glasses and balancing a camera and a bulky case labeled Crime Scene. He got right to the business of cataloging the scene while the detective focused on June and me.

"Good evening, ladies. I'm Lucas Rains. I'll be handling this investigation." He was about to extend his hand in greeting, but pulled it back and instead retrieved a pen and notebook from an inside jacket pocket. He was ready to get started. June and I introduced ourselves, and Detective Rains wrote down our information.

"I need to know exactly what happened from the time you left the dining room until you discovered Mr. Truffle. Take your time. Don't leave anything out no matter how insignificant it might seem."

Since I'd spent the long minutes before the detective got here going over every last detail, I was able to give a cohesive and comprehensive account of the events. The only thing tripping me up was the sight of the crime scene investigator circling Truffle's body and the clicking sound of his camera magnified in the enclosed space. June left the talking to me but nodded in agreement after every point I made.

When the lab technician pulled a long silver probe from his case, June and I flinched simultaneously. I had watched enough TV to know he was about to determine Truffle's time of death, but it didn't make it any easier to witness.

The detective picked up on what was happening and came to our rescue. "Duncan, would you please step outside and call the medical examiner? We're almost finished here."

The young man didn't argue. He pulled out his cell phone and left. I had a feeling Detective Rains was used to people following his orders.

"That's it," I said. "I've told you every detail I can think of." Rains flipped his notebook closed and clicked his pen. I ended with, "Oh, why couldn't I have just waited until tomorrow to ask for a doggie bag for my husband?"

"It's okay, ma'am."

I had to stop him there. "Please call me Francie. Ma'am just makes everything sound worse."

"All right then, Francie. I was about to say it's probably a good thing you found Mr. Truffle when you did. Otherwise, he probably wouldn't have been missed until tomorrow afternoon. According to what I learned from some crew members, breakfast isn't served aboard the ship so the chef had tonight and most of tomorrow morning off. The killer would have had plenty of time to tamper with the crime scene, plant or remove evidence, move the body, or who knows what else."

This again made me think we might be on borrowed time. The killer could be in the hall right now, waiting to see who the nosy witnesses, and perhaps his next victims, might be.

I was relieved when Detective Rains wrapped things up. I was getting anxious to leave. "I think I have everything I need from you for now. Why don't you go on back to your room while Duncan and I finish up here? I'll check back with you tomorrow morning in case you recall anything else."

Finally. I felt cold and drained and didn't put up any resistance. June promised she'd accompany me, smiled agreeably, and added, "Shouldn't Captain Blackhart be here? I can track him down if you'd like. I think he might be participating in the events over at the park."

"Leave the detective work to me and the department, if you don't mind." Rains flipped quickly through his notes and continued. " You said you were a reporter, June? Don't be getting any bright ideas about getting involved in all of this. The best thing you both can do now is go to your room and try to get some rest. I'll take it from here."

"You got it, Detective." June gave Rains a mock salute.

Was she flirting with him? Under different circumstances, I'd be uninterested in her behavior. Even considering her budding romance with Jack, flirting was as much a part of June's identity as the ever-changing streak of color in her blond pixie hair. For now, though, I thought it might be mildly inappropriate but decided to let it go. People coped with stress in countless ways. We did as we were told and remained quiet until we got back to my stateroom and closed the door.

"Time to follow orders, Francie. Sit down and relax," June said, nudging me toward a chair. She must have noticed my hands were starting to tremble. "I'll fix us a drink." She pulled a bottle of wine from her overnight bag, set it on the bedside table, and continued rummaging through her things. "I must not have packed an opener. I'm sure you have one stashed in your purse. Toss it here, would you?"

I stared at her. Was she rubbing it in on purpose?

"Oh, hey. I'm really sorry. With everything else that's happened, I almost forgot about the whole bird thing. You've had one heck of a day."

That was an understatement. She fetched me a glass and the complimentary bottle of water from the dresser. "I'll pop down to the gift shop and buy myself one of those overpriced souvenir wine keys. I'll be right back. Put your feet up, take some breaths, and try to clear your head." She grabbed her purse and headed out.

Before I had my shoes off, there was a knock on the door. "Back already? Did you forget your key?"

I peeked out the peephole but didn't see my friend. Instead I saw a crewmember with a tray containing two delicious-looking cocktails. He was just about to knock again when I opened the door.

"Mrs. Egg?"

"It's Egge, but yes, that's me."

"Captain Blackhart sends these with his regrets." The boy entered and set the tray on the dresser. "He apologizes for your troubles this evening and assures you he will do everything he can to make it up to you. If there's anything you need, you can call the number on this card. It's the captain's personal line."

"Well, thank you. Is the captain talking to Detective Rains?"

"I wouldn't know, ma'am. Is there anything else?"

"No. Thanks for bringing the drinks. They look fabulous." There was an awkward pause as I realized the young man was waiting for a tip. I had no cash, June wasn't around, and I didn't feel like explaining the whole bird situation. "Tell me your name, and I'll make sure you're taken care of tomorrow when my husband arrives."

"That won't be necessary, ma'am. You have a good evening." And with that, he was gone.

"Who was the pirate sneaking out of your room?" June was back before I could check the mirror for wrinkles. Why was everyone suddenly calling me ma'am?

"He works here. He brought us a special delivery from Captain Blackhart—some drinks along with his apologies. Is that standard protocol when someone finds a dead body aboard a ship?"

"I don't know, but things just got even more complicated."

"What are you talking about?"

"When I went to pay for my overpriced wine opener, I discovered my wallet was missing. I had it when I checked in at the Sparrow's Nest. That's the last time I can be certain of having it, so either I left it at the inn, or someone snagged it between then and now."

"Either is possible," I said. "There are so many people around, and obviously not all of them are good Samaritans.

There's a murderer somewhere close by. A pickpocket is small potatoes by comparison."

June plopped herself into the second chair and put her feet up on the bed. "This day sure hasn't turned out how I envisioned it."

"I couldn't agree more. We've both had more than our share of misfortune today. I wish Hamm were here. He'd know what to do."

"Speaking of Hamm, you don't think we need a lawyer, do you? Do you think Detective Rains suspects we were involved? Did you notice how good-looking he is?"

"Yes, June, I noticed. And trust me. He noticed you too. Unfortunately, I think he was distracted by poor Mr. Truffle on the floor."

The mention of the chef made it all real again. The room's atmosphere sunk into a cocoon of gloom. I felt afraid and sad for this man I didn't even know. After a moment of quiet reflection, I raised my martini glass in a toast to Chef Truffle.

After one sip, my mood brightened a little. "I have to give it to Captain Blackhart. I'm pretty sure this is the best drink I've ever tasted."

I looked closely at the glass before taking another sip. There was a bright red strawberry floating in its center. The pink puree was sweet and cold, and the taste of chocolate kissed my thirsty lips. Uh-oh. I could choose to indulge in the captain's gift even if it seemed like an odd response to finding a dead body, but June's choices were limited. She could drink it, swell up, and break out in severe hives, or put it down and save a trip to the clinic.

"June, stop. There's choco..."

"I know. It's swirled on the inside of the glass. I didn't see it at first. Looks like you get a double tonight."

"I'm sorry."

"Hey, it's not your fault. Go ahead and enjoy them both. I think I'll take a walk and get some air. Who knows, maybe I'll run into someone who has a corkscrew I can borrow. I'll leave my phone so you can call Hamm without being attached to a cord. I'd rather not listen to your half of a personal phone call anyway. I'm sure he'll be wanting to console you, and you never know where that might lead."

I blushed, but I didn't deny it could happen. June smiled, tossed her phone on the bed, and closed the door softly on her way out.

I finished the drinks alone in the beautiful stateroom and talked at length to my husband. Starting at the beginning, I told him everything—from having to put up with Marla Fuller, to my encounter with the crazy parrot, the ship, the food, and finally the early demise of Chef Truffle. Putting the day into words was helping as much or more as the effect of the complimentary cocktails.

Slowly, my jangled nerves were soothed by Hamm's comforting voice. He assured me I would be safe and reminded me to stay in the cabin. Things would be better in the morning. I listened as he talked about his own day. He tried to keep the conversation light, but even through the haze of alcohol, I recognized the edge of worry in his voice. He didn't say it, but I knew he felt guilty about staying at the marina instead of being with me tonight. There was no way to have predicted today's events, and both of us agreed it was a good thing I had June with me.

"Try to sleep now, Francie. I'll be with you first thing in the morning."

"Thanks Hamm. I'm so much better now. I can make it until I see you tomorrow. I love you."

"I love you too. Goodnight."

I tried to wait up for June to get back from her walk, but the lamplight seemed so bright, and I swear it was starting to put off heat. I was getting very uncomfortable and thought I might be having an anxiety attack. I tried to slow my racing heart and clear my mind by taking long calming breaths. Finally, I got up and washed two ibuprofen down with a glass of water. Climbing into bed, I pulled the covers up to my chin, closed my burning eyes and let sleep have its way with me.

Chapter 4

"Something's wrong! I can barely see." Swiping my hand across my face, I encountered plastic. Moving my fingertips to my temples, I touched a familiar metal and rhinestone hinge embellishment. "June, did you put these glasses on me? What the heck?"

June fell out of the desk chair with a loud thump. "What are you talking about, Francie?" She stood up gingerly, rubbing her back and bending from side to side.

"I just woke up and felt really weird. My head hurts and my eyes are burning." I sat up in bed, took the glasses off, and inspected them. "These are my sunglasses but I don't remember putting them on. And why would I? Who wears sunglasses in bed?"

June was paying no attention to my predicament. Instead, she picked up a magazine and waved it around her head.

"June, help me out here. I can't remember what happened."

"Forget about your night vision for a minute, Francie. There's a bird in the room! Why is that thing in here? Get your butt out of bed and help me get rid of it!"

"What are you talking about?" I was still trying to figure out why I was wearing sunglasses, but June was dancing around waving her magazine like a flag twirler on the fifty-yard line, making my mental task all but impossible. "Put that thing down, will you? You'll throw your back out. And why were you sleeping in the chair?"

June swatted her magazine dangerously close to my head. What the heck? I realized she wasn't kidding about the bird. It screeched, swooped low across the bed, and flapped its rainbow wings before perching atop the pole lamp in the corner of the room.

Sitting there in the middle of the bed, trying to clear the cobwebs from my brain, I had a flashback to a childhood memory. My older brother had a pet parakeet named, of all things, Pretty Boy. James knew I was afraid of it when he let it out of the cage to fly around the living room, and he used this bit of information to torture me. It worked. One day, I decided to get my revenge. While Pretty Boy preened himself in his cage, I threw crayons at him. Most of them ended up scattered about the carpet, but my aim improved with practice, and I managed to land four or five through the wrought iron bars into his domain. He must have thought I was sending him peace offerings. Being the birdbrain he was, the parakeet munched on the colorful treats until he flopped over. When my mother came into the room, she found Pretty Boy on his back with his tiny yellow feet pointed straight in the air and me sprawled on the floor engrossed in my favorite coloring book. She was not impressed with my accomplishment. If it wasn't for Mom's quick actions, my brother might have lost his pet that day. I tell myself Pretty Boy would have gotten over his bellyache. I try to feel contrition for my actions. I still do not like birds.

June had stopped her maniacal dance and was glaring at the bird on the lamp pole. Another image popped into my head—that of a frightening, soul sucking bird rasping "Nevermore" for all eternity. I shook my head vigorously in an attempt to banish all the crazy thoughts, settling at last on June and following her gaze to the corner of the room.

I swear the parrot was looking right at me. "You stole my heart. Stole my heart."

June lowered her makeshift weapon. "I think Pretty Boy is flirting with you, Francie."

That was the final straw. "This is wrong in so many ways. First of all, I'm taken. Secondly, he's a *bird*. And most importantly, I hate him! I hate birds, period, and this one stole my purse, not my heart!"

"Hate is a harsh word, Francie. Maybe he's trying to apologize. He didn't actually steal your purse—you threw it at him, remember?"

"So, now you're best friends? You were just trying to whack it—a much better idea in my opinion. Hold still. I'm calling the staff to come and get the vile thing out of here." I reached for the phone on the bedside table and dialed the service number.

"He is a pretty boy, don't you think? Now that he's sitting still, I feel kind of sorry for him. He lost his master, and he's probably hungry. Do you have any crackers in your...oh...sorry!"

I still wasn't feeling the love. My purse was gone, my eyes were sore, and I had a dull headache. There were unanswered questions about last night to deal with. It couldn't be a hangover. I hadn't had that much to drink, so I was probably dehydrated. I remembered the horror of tripping over Chef Truffle in the galley, and then I remembered Hamm promising me things would be better in the morning. If this was better, I shuddered to think what the rest of the day had in store.

While waiting for the extraction team, I smoothed the covers over the bed, more to erase the evidence of what happened than to reduce the housekeeper's workload. June scrolled through her phone messages just in case there was something from Hamm about when he'd be arriving. No missed calls or messages showed on her screen, but it was still early.

There was a knock on the door. A young man dressed in full pirate regalia stood in the doorway. "Good morning, Mrs. Egge. I hope your first night aboard the *Angel's Trumpet* was enjoyable."

I thought that was an odd choice of words. "Thanks. It was memorable, to say the least."

"I was informed that Pretty Boy paid you a visit this morning. He's a friendly fellow, isn't he? We need to give the rest of the guests some time to get to know him, so I'll have to take him with me. I'm sure you'll get another chance to hang out this weekend."

Was this guy for real? It was hard to tell. He seemed genuinely cheerful, and he made no mention of Chef Truffle's untimely demise. I wondered if the crew was even aware of last night's tragedy. None of them expected to see him until lunchtime, so as Detective Rains mentioned last night, he wouldn't be missed for a while.

"The captain asked me to pass along an invitation. You and the other guests are invited to a special buffet breakfast over at The Plank. The price is included in your prize package."

"Thanks for the information and the invitation, but not to be rude, could you please take care of the uninvited guest. I promise you I don't want to prevent the other guests from enjoying him as much as we have." I opened the door wider and stepped aside to give our visitor full access to the room. One whistle from pirate boy and the parrot was out of the room, and with any luck, out of my life for good.

June shut the door behind the bird and the boy and locked it. She paced across the room and back several times, nodding her head. A stranger would have found her actions disquieting, but I recognized she was in thinking mode. Finally, she sat on the edge of the bed and put her hands between her knees.

"Do you think it's true?"

I wasn't up to speed with her specific thoughts, so I had to ask. "Do I think what's true?"

"The breakfast. Was it on the itinerary? I don't remember seeing anything about breakfast being served at another location. Did the captain really have this planned, or was it something Detective Rains cooked up to get everyone off the boat so he could poke around?"

I thought about it. "I don't know. Does it really matter? Either way, we get a free breakfast, which by the way, is a good thing considering neither one of us currently has any cash.

"Touché," June said on her way to the shower.

While June got ready, I opened my suitcase and organized my things in the dresser, making sure to leave the top drawer empty for Hamm. Carefully choosing my clothes for the day gave me something to occupy my mind other than a murderer on the loose and a bird intent on driving me insane. I settled on my white crepe Barbarossa blouse. Its plunging V-neckline with frills around the edges and down the front gave it the perfect feminine pirate flair. Loose fitting sleeves with a frill at the wrists added an extra authentic touch without being too warm or constrictive. Cropped, wide-legged, black trousers, black leather boots and belt with silver accents, and big, silver hoop earrings completed my ensemble. I let my dark, wavy hair hang loose around my shoulders. I looked pretty and pirate-y, if I do say so myself.

Admiring my completed ensemble in the mirror, I thought about the dreams I'd been having lately. I felt myself slipping back into the persona of Rose. I didn't even know if she was a real person, a character from a historical romance, or even a ghost trying to get my attention. Her presence felt so real, and for a moment I wanted nothing more than to be transported in time to her world—my world.

"Let's get going. I'm starving!" My friend was unaware she had pulled me back from my fantasy even though for a second I was sad she had broken the spell.

June had chosen royal blue capris, a stretchy white T-shirt with blue trim, and red tennis shoes for the day. She hadn't packed to play pirate, yet she looked perfect—right down to the red and blue streak in her spiky blond halo of hair.

I had to retrieve my sunglasses from under the bed covers before we exited our room and made our way toward the main deck. My eyes were still oddly sensitive, even to the dim light of the ship's hallway. Passing the galley door with its carved parrot inlay sent a shiver of recollection down my spine, and I picked up my pace, anxious to get out of the belly of the ship. I stopped short when we left the top deck and moved out of the shade of the massive sails onto the shore. My eyes stung from the bright sun, and it already felt stifling hot for so early in the morning. Maybe I should have reconsidered the boots and chosen my strappy sandals instead. Oh well, I could change after breakfast.

We walked the short distance to The Plank, a beautiful three-storied landmark recognized as South Bass Island's most popular eatery, where a private buffet was set up on the upper deck. I had to show my Winner's Circle pass in order for us to enjoy the unlimited quantities of food and drink catered for us by the island's most famous restaurant. Since Hamm hadn't arrived yet, June could use his card. I missed him though and resolved to call him right after breakfast.

When I saw the buffet, I decided to forgo my diet once again and indulge to my heart's content. I was craving carbs, and I was at the right place. All the dishes were labeled with creative names. I walked the length of the buffet before helping myself to piles of pancakes, eggs overboard, and boats of oats. Then there were the side items like maple rum syrup, juicy fruit gems, and mulled apple-rum cider.

I didn't feel guilty about any of my choices when I saw what was on June's plate. For someone who was a size two soaking wet, she could eat dessert three times a day. Her metabolism was in constant overdrive, and although I wasn't technically jealous, a tiny bit of me hoped that someday it would catch up with her, and she would experience my constant struggle to maintain my fairly average figure.

We found a table with a perfect view of the lake, and I maneuvered toward the one seat that was in complete shade.

I thought it felt unseasonably hot, and I asked myself again whether I should have opted for an outfit consisting of less fabric. Looking around, I noticed almost everyone was dressed in layers appropriate for early September. June was shrugging into a little white sweater she pulled out of her shoulder bag and maneuvering her chair so she had better access to the warmth of the sun.

I settled in for our morning repast and tried not to groan with pleasure as I dug into my bounty. The only thing beside the temperature distracting me from the pleasure of my meal was the sight of a certain parrot staring at me from his perch on the deck rail. The sun behind him made his jewel-toned feathers luminous. He would look stunning on the glossy cover of a travel magazine. Despite his good looks, I had to wonder why the wretched thing was dogging me. It was unnatural and more than a little unsettling.

A shrill whistle behind me snapped me out of my musings over the motives of the ship's mascot. "Come to Captain, my Pretty Boy!" Captain Blackhart stepped into view, bowed with a flourish, and stood at attention. Pretty Boy did not do as the captain bid. Instead, he flew straight to our table and settled himself on the back of my chair. He leisurely preened his feathers, looking like he had no intention of going anywhere soon. So much for sharing him with the other guests. Maybe June was right. Maybe he did have a crush on me.

"Mind if I join you folks?" Captain Blackhart reached out his hand to Pretty Boy who promptly turned away from him and squawked, "Heart of Black. Heart of Black."

"Pull up a chair, Captain. Of course, we'd love for you to join us," I responded. I then gave Pretty Boy a look I hadn't used since reprimanding disrespectful teenagers in drama class.

He sat across from me, keeping Pretty Boy in his sight. "That parrot says the darndest things, doesn't he? It's interesting how he uses his limited vocabulary in ways that actually seem to make sense. Sometimes, it's almost as if he's deliberately talking to people."

"You call it interesting. I find it more unsettling."

"In any case, he seems to have formed an attachment to you, Francesca. Please let me know if he becomes too much of a bother, and I'll have him taken care of."

"Thank you, Captain. I might feel differently if we'd met under better circumstances." I retold the story of Pretty Boy versus purse for Blackhart's benefit even though he stopped listening to me as soon as he laid eyes on June. I reminded him she was my temporary companion, noting she'd be heading back to the Sparrow's Nest Inn as soon as Hamm arrived. He knew that. He wasn't worried about me taking advantage of my guest allotment. He just hadn't expected her to still be here this morning, but now that she was, he wasn't going to pass up another opportunity to get to know her.

Blackhart reached for June's hand, never taking his smoky, kohl-rimmed eyes off her sweet pixie face. Oh, jeez. It was happening again, and as always, she seemed oblivious to the phenomenon, making the moment sizzle all the more.

"So, Captain, have you learned anything more about your chef? Will Detective Rains be back to question the Fullers?" I tried my best to break the spell, but June was still smiling, and Blackhart was still ignoring me.

Pretty Boy came to the rescue. Maybe he was my friend after all. He flapped his wings behind my head, rose into the air, and began circling and swooping, faster and faster. Blackhart looked at me like he was seeing me for the first time. "What did you say about the Fullers? Did they say something to you?"

"No, not exactly. It's just that last night I saw Liz..." The rest of my sentence was cut off by a scream.

Marla Fuller was gaping at the scene unfolding near the buffet table. Her daughter screamed again as Pretty Boy flew directly at her. She raised her purse. I was transfixed. It was a cross between an out-of-body experience and déjà vu. What was it with this bird? Liz's handbag missed its mark, just like mine had. But, unlike mine, her bag landed on the solid wood deck. Its contents spilled crazily around her feet but could eventually be retrieved and reordered. Captain Blackhart jumped to his feet to assist Liz with her things. As he was handing her wallet back to her, Pretty Boy finally decided to bless the pirate with his companionship and landed on his shoulder.

"Give it Back. Give it Back." Was the parrot having guilt pangs for causing another handbag disaster?

Liz accepted the oversized green leather billfold. There were slips of paper and plastic cards sticking out from every opening. If her wallet was anything like my daughter's, one would be hard pressed to find any certified dollar bills among the jumble. Paying with cash was becoming a thing of the past among the younger generation. "Thank you, Captain," she said, and got back to the job of scooping up her scattered belongings.

"My apologies to you, Miss Fuller. Our bird here has been getting into more mischief than usual this weekend. Please call me if he bothers you again." He handed her a familiar-looking card.

Maybe my luck was turning. Maybe Pretty Boy would trade me in for Liz and become her weekend friend and protector. His loyalty to Captain Blackhart was short-lived. He screeched and flew off, leaving the chaos he had created without so much as a backward glance.

Chapter 5

June picked up her fork. "I think the show is over, and my breakfast is getting cold." She returned to the task in front of her with renewed focus.

I was glad to see June was acting like herself again, but I realized I wasn't as hungry as I thought I was. I was anxious to talk to Hamm, my eyes were burning, and my eye drops, of course, were in my handbag at the bottom of the lake.

"June, can I borrow your phone? I want to find out what time Hamm will be getting here."

She slid it across the table without looking up from her plate. I admired her concentration. I walked across the deck to the rail, so I could look out over the harbor while talking to my husband. He picked up on the first ring. An unexpected tear landed on my cheek when I heard his voice, and as I brushed it away, I was surprised at the comfort the long-distance contact brought me.

"Hi, Francie. I was just about to call you. How are things this morning? Everything back to normal?"

"It depends on what you mean by normal." I detailed my morning encounters with Pretty Boy, told him about June's missing wallet, and described the free breakfast buffet. "I really miss you, Hamm. Will you be here in time to buy me lunch?"

He hesitated. "About that. I'm afraid I have some bad news."

"What? I can't take any more bad news. Are you okay? Did something happen to the boat?"

"I'm fine. Our boat is fine."

"What then? If everything is fine, what's the bad news?"

"It's the houseboat."

"June's boat? What could be wrong with June's boat? It doesn't even run." June kept her old houseboat at Beacon Pointe in the slip right across from ours. It never left the dock but was perfect as a summer cottage in a prime location.

"Honey, let me talk." Hamm waited a second to make sure I wasn't going to butt in again before he continued. "First let me say it's not a total disaster."

"A total..." I clamped my hand over my mouth.

"It's still floating, but it needs some repairs. Early this morning, just after sunrise, the EPA guys were back checking for damages or other contaminated areas. Since I was awake, I went outside to see what was going on. I noticed the houseboat leaning at an unnatural angle, and when I went over to take a closer look, I found a hole in the hull. I think someone shot off a flare last night and it hit the side of June's boat. Honestly, if I hadn't noticed it when I did, the whole thing would be underwater by now."

"Oh, no. Should we come back? What should I tell June?"

"Listen, honey. The worst of it's over. There's no need for either of you to return. The marina repair service vacuumed the water out. They'll be back later this afternoon to pull the boat out. It'll need to be repaired on land. I'll stay here and make sure it all happens. If it's okay with you, June can take my place for whatever activities the weekend organizers have planned for today, at least until I get there. I'd feel better making sure this is handled right. Do you think she'll be okay with that? I know she's there for her own assignment, but she's usually pretty flexible when it comes to location. And by the sound of it, you're probably providing her with some added color for her article. On a more serious note, though, I don't want you to be alone. You're safer together."

I knew Hamm was right. He would make sure things got done, and I knew he'd never be able to relax if he left without knowing they were. He also knew the only person other than him I would feel safe with was my best friend. In spite of Hamm and June's volatile relationship, there was no denying we had each other's backs.

"Oh, Hamm. June will be grateful, I'm sure. She knows how you are with boats. I'm also sure she'll hang out with me until you can get here. I'll just miss you, that's all. Well, that and the problem of neither of us having any cash or credit cards."

"Why not ask the captain, or whoever is in charge, if you can get a voucher or a loan or something to tide you over. June will probably find her wallet at her hotel, and she can help you out until I get there."

"Okay. We'll manage. Just get here as soon as you can. Love you."

"Love you too, and see you soon."

After ending the call, I stared at the blank phone screen, not wanting to break the connection right away. When I left my post at the rail, I saw Captain Blackhart walking toward the table where June was finishing her breakfast, but was relieved when Zach beat him there and plopped down in the seat I had vacated. "What's new? Anything? The food looks great. Mind if I sit here?"

He was uncharacteristically chatty and didn't wait for answers, but set his camera at his place and strode to the buffet to help himself. I got to the table in time to watch him juggle several plates of food and a mug while trying to lower himself into his chair without spilling anything on his expensive equipment. Meanwhile, Bradley slid into the chair beside Zach and set a steaming cup of black coffee in front of him. I pulled up a chair, gave the guys a cursory greeting, and relayed the news from Hamm. June seemed more annoyed than upset about her houseboat and easily agreed to be Hamm's stand-in until he arrived. We discussed the money problem, and both Zach and Bradley offered to loan us some cash for the weekend. Things were far from ideal, but at least they were looking up.

Blackhart had finished pacing. He cleared his throat and addressed the group from the center of the deck where he could be seen by all. "I see everyone is here." He must have had a microphone clipped beneath the ruffles of his shirt because his voice carried easily across the space occupied by our private party. "I want to welcome you all once again, invite you to enjoy your breakfast, and ask for your attention for a brief moment."

June switched her attentive gaze from the remains of her breakfast to the captain, ready to hear what he had to say.

"It is with a heavy heart that I pass this information along to all of you. Some of you already know, and others, I'm sure have heard rumors. A good man, personal friend, and chef beyond measure passed away last night in the galley of the *Angel's Trumpet*. His death was not from natural causes."

I heard the intake of breath from several people behind us. Obviously, not everyone had heard the news.

"The police are investigating and will leave no stone unturned until we get to the bottom of this," Blackhart continued. "Please be cooperative and forthcoming. If you saw or heard something last night, no matter how insignificant it might seem right now, please tell me or one of the investigators. We are honored to have Detective Lucas Rains here, and he has been appointed lead investigator on this case." The captain nodded in the detective's direction and gave him a subtle cue to stand. I hadn't noticed him slip into a seat at a table behind ours. Rains raised himself about halfway from his seat then sat back down looking uncomfortable.

"As grim as this situation is, I encourage you all to try and enjoy your time here on the island. This year's Pirate Fest is destined to be one for the history books. Be careful as you go about your days, but don't be afraid to have some fun as well."

Pretty Boy was back, squawking and flapping, and calling out, "Trouble for Truffle. Trouble for Truffle."

As soon as Blackhart was out of sight, Marla Fuller bolted across the deck, making a beeline for the table where Detective Rains was sitting with some other paying guests. She gave me a snotty side-glance before stopping in front of the detective and launching into a rant.

"Detective Rains is it? I know who you're looking for! Last night at the opening ceremonies in the park, I saw them. I know it must have been them. I told Elisabeth there was something criminal going on."

"Slow down, ma'am. Who and what did you see exactly?" Rains raised his hand, trying to focus on the woman's excited rambling. "Can you start from the beginning?"

"It was two of the pirates from the ship. They were arguing loudly. I thought the one was going to run the other one through with his sword." They kept talking about getting rid of the bag. I'm sure they must have been talking about Chef Truffle. What else could it be?"

"Ma'am..."

"Please stop calling me that. The name's Marla."

"I'm sorry, ma...I mean Marla, but how can you be sure these pirates you saw came from the *Angel's Trumpet*? There were pirates all over the park last night for the opening ceremonies of Pirate Fest."

"Well," she backpedaled, "I guess I can't be one hundred percent sure, but it must have been them. They were up to no good. You need to go arrest them."

Detective Rains was making a valiant effort to remain calm and polite. "Okay, Marla, just tell me exactly what these two looked like. Better yet, did you get their names?"

"Well, you know, they looked like pirates. One wore a bandana and an eye patch over his left eye. No, wait. It was his right." She hesitated for a second. When she spoke next, her voice had raised at least an octave in pitch. "Why are you trying to discredit me? Why don't you go do your job?"

I heard the whole thing and gave Detective Rains credit for keeping a straight face. He assured Marla he would look into the pirate lead, excused himself, and headed back toward town.

While I was eavesdropping on Marla's improbable story, June was trying out name options for our treasure hunt team.

"What do you think about The Looters, or the Paradise Loungers, or The Booty Hunters?" She was reading from a list from a blog on her phone.

I shot her a look. "I'm not too sure about any of those. Let's head over to the sign-up table, and maybe we can come up with something clever."

According to Mr. Thorn's directions last night, we needed to have a team name ready before we checked in with the first mate. As skeptical as I was about this treasure hunt, I was glad we had an organized event to keep us distracted while Chef Truffle's murder was being investigated.

As I was thinking, someone whispered in my ear. I whipped around to see who it was, but no one was there. The mid-morning sun was blazing in my eyes, but I was sure of the words I heard—the Black Roses. Whether it was my imagination, a ghost from the past, or heat stroke, I liked it. "Let's go with the Black Roses. What do you think, June?"

"I love it—the Black Roses it is."

June slid her phone back into her pocket. "Maybe we can channel your imaginary friend Rose to help us win this thing. I won't even be jealous of you spending more time with your notes on her than with me."

June's words made me vaguely uncomfortable. Imaginary friends were for lonely children and adults with mental issues, not smart, competent winners of national recipe contests. Maybe I should keep Rose to myself from now on.

I printed our team name in the sign-in book, and we were officially the Black Roses. The first mate handed me a plastic bag, and wished us success on the treasure hunt.

"What's in the bag, Francie? Let me have a look." June took the bag from me and tore it open. She pulled out a sheet of paper with the rules and a timeline printed on it, two black rubber wristbands, and a gold envelope sealed with a red wax stamp.

"Look, Francie, it must be fate," she said, holding up the black bracelets. "Black bracelets for the Black Roses."

I took one from her and slipped it on my wrist. "So what's the clue?" We might as well get moving before everyone else is on to it."

June slid a ruby red nail under the wax seal, opened the envelope, and pulled out a weathered parchment card. She read the clue silently, bit her lower lip, and then read it again, aloud this time.

"When young, I am sweet in the sun. When middle-aged, I fuel your adventure. When old, I am valued more than ever."

June pulled her phone back out of her pocket and tapped on the screen. "I'm not coming up with anything through a quick Internet search." Her comments were in sync with her tapping.

"Do you have another idea?" I asked. "It looks like Zach and Bradley are heading to the golf cart rental kiosk. Maybe they figured it out already. It must be somewhere out of walking range. Should we go rent a cart now? June? What do you think? How are we going to pay for it? Who is going to leave their ID and be responsible for the rental? Even with a few bucks from the guys, we still can't rent a golf cart without a driver's license or credit card. Do you know the answer yet?"

I sucked in my breath. What the heck had come over me? I'm not generally so high strung. It must be a side effect of losing my purse in the lake. My bag, and all its contents, was my security blanket. I'm sure if I had it with me, I would be able to figure out the clue. At least I would have had something to help me think. The last time I was stuck on a problem, I reached into my purse and pulled out a mini bottle of champagne. I popped the top and came up with the answer—Jack-in-the-Box. I don't recall the question, but I've concluded that my purse had a way of helping me out in stressful situations, perhaps as a thank you for hauling its weight around. Too bad it was now another sunken treasure at the bottom of Lake Erie. I could surely use another mini-champagne inspiration.

"Wait! That's it."

"What's what?" June was looking at me strangely.

"Wine." I stood there triumphantly with my hands on my hips.

June whispered behind her hand to me, "It's still a little early for wine, don't you think, Francie?"

"I don't want wine. Wine is the answer. The superpowers of my lost handbag helped me figure it out even from the bottom of the lake."

June was starting to look worried. I needed to explain before I got committed and hauled off to the ship's mental ward—if there was a mental ward on a pirate ship. "Don't you get it? The answer to the riddle is wine. Grapes grow on the vines sweet in the sun. Then when they're made into wine, they fuel people's fun. And finally, the older a wine is, the more it goes up in value."

"Oh, well it's rather simple when you put it that way."

I was doing a happy dance in my head. I hooked my left arm through June's and led her back toward the ship. We had to get to Heinemann's Winery and Crystal Cave, but I needed to change into something cooler and less constrictive if we were going to be hopping on and off a golf cart all afternoon tracking down answers to clues and riddles. My tall boots looked nice, but I was ready for my flip-flops.

We were almost to our room when a man's shadow crossed our path, causing me to jump sideways. Keeping at bay thoughts of a murderer lurking in dark corners waiting for his opportunity to eliminate any threat of discovery was easier said than done. When I realized who it was, I pushed my fear back down into my gut and tried to recover a semblance of casual nonchalance.

"Hi, ladies. I was just heading to my cabin to pick up our itinerary. Did you get yours yet?"

"No, Zach, we haven't been inside yet. Where's Bradley? I thought I saw you guys heading to the golf cart rental place."

I couldn't tell if he was acting strangely or if my hyperactive imagination was throwing suspicion at everyone. Maybe I just got his name wrong and he was trying to be polite by not correcting me. It happens to twins often—even twins who look nothing alike. He shifted his feet uneasily and glanced down the hall.

"Oh, my brother went on ahead to rent the cart. I came back here to grab the itinerary in case there was something important on it. Was there? Did you read it yet?"

"Um, no. As I just said, we haven't been inside the room yet."

"Oh, sorry. See you later, gotta go." He ran down the hall looking back over his shoulder as he ran. It was a miracle he didn't fall on his face.

"That was weird," June said, picking up our copy of the day's itinerary in the entry hall. It must have been slipped under the cabin door while we were at breakfast. She read it aloud to me while I scurried around the room, slinging off my pirate ensemble and pulling on a more serviceable outfit. My coral tank top and coral and gray print skort would serve me better than flowing pants, flouncy sleeves, and tall boots. At the last minute, I opted for my white sneakers instead of my flip-flops, thinking they'd be more practical for a day of riddle solving and investigation.

Chapter 6

"So, about the golf cart." I hoped June had a plan for acquiring our transportation because without ID, I couldn't think of anything.

"I've got this," she announced while retrieving her phone. She was giving her pants pocket a run for the money. "I've got my press pass saved in an app. It gives me some access privileges, including transportation. Let's see if it works for golf cart rental. There's a barcode, they can scan which should contain all the information they need."

When we got to the cart rental window, I held my breath and crossed my fingers while June handed her phone over to the rental agent. He didn't even look up at her as he scanned her code. She signed on the dotted line, took the key, and stepped aside for the next customer in line.

"That was too easy," I said, sliding onto the front seat beside my designated driver. June usually left the driving to me, preferring to take in the scenery and use the time to update her notes on whatever project she was working on. Being the driver, forced her to sit still and concentrate—something she rarely did by choice. Until I got my credentials back, however, we'd have to remain in role reversal.

"Yeah. It's a good thing my wallet was the only thing I misplaced last night. It's crazy how we've all become so attached to our cell phones."

"True, but also very fortunate. Who would have believed ten years ago that you could store important documents like your driver's license and insurance cards on a phone? Talking is probably the least important function to most people. I'm feeling pretty lost without mine. Thanks for letting me use yours to call Hamm. I'll need to borrow it again later to see when he'll be able to get here."

"No problem. What are friends for? But before we head to the winery, do you mind if we make a quick stop at the Sparrow's Nest? Maybe we can check one mystery off our list if my wallet is waiting for me in the lost and found."

Before I could give my consent, I was startled by someone hopping into the backseat of our golf cart. It was the detective.

"Good morning ladies. I'm glad I caught you before you headed out. Where are you going?"

I regained my composure before I answered. "Good morning to you, Detective. You startled me. Do you make it a habit to jump into people's vehicles unannounced?"

"Just doing my job. We don't have much staff on the islands to begin with, and the holiday weekend is stretching everyone pretty thin. By the way, I spoke with Jack Morgan last night. He was surprised to hear your names in conjunction with my murder investigation."

What could either of us say to that? I had no idea how much information Jack had shared with Detective Raines, and decided the less fuel added to that fire the better off we'd be.

June must have agreed with me. She skipped over the topic like it was never mentioned.

"We're going to the Sparrow's Nest Inn to see if anyone turned in my wallet. I misplaced it last night. After that, we're headed to the winery."

"A little early in the day to start drinking, don't you think?"

I glimpsed evidence of a sense of humor behind the detective's serious brown eyes. I guessed him to be around the same age as my husband. His physique was a cross between a runner and a bodybuilder, and his snug tee shirt made it hard to concentrate on his official status even with the words Lake Erie PD stretched across his chest. There was no wedding ring on his left hand.

"We're not going there to drink." I jumped back into the conversation. "It's part of the treasure hunt we're doing. We solved our first clue and need to collect our token and get the next riddle. Is there something you need, Detective, because we're already falling behind."

"I'd like to ask you some more questions about last night."

June pulled out of the rental lot and bumped our golf cart into traffic. "Feel free to ride along. We can talk as we go."

Now it was Detective Rains's turn to look startled. He was unfamiliar with June's habit of blurting out whatever was on her mind or her take-charge attitude. To some people she could come off as rude, but I knew how her mind worked. Whatever the case, he remained in the golf cart, but he didn't say anything during the short trip to the Sparrow's Nest Inn. June switched off the ignition, hopped out of the cart, and strode up the front walk before he uttered his first word.

I turned in my seat to face our spur-of-the-moment guest and pulled a questioning role reversal on him. "So, what was it you wanted to talk about, Detective Rains? You said you had more questions. I haven't remembered anything else since last night, and I thought you were very thorough then. Did you find new evidence?"

I think I surprised him, but his rebuttal was cut short by June's voice, which carried from across the street. Rains and I watched her leave the hotel engaged in a lively conversation with a pirate. The young man's clothing was professional quality, not a flimsy costume purchased from one of the dozens of tourist shops taking full advantage of the spirit of Pirate Fest. June waved goodbye to the lad as she bounced back into the driver's seat.

"That was fast," I said. I could have been referring to either the speed in which she conducted her business or how quickly she attracted eligible young men.

"My wallet wasn't there. They checked in the lost and found and behind the front desk. I gave them my info in case someone turns it in, but at this point, I'm not getting my hopes up."

"And who's your new friend?" I inquired.

"I didn't catch his name. I complimented him on his awesome pirate outfit, and he told me he was an actor doing a gig on the *Angel's Trumpet* for the weekend. I think he might have been the same guy who came to our room this morning, but then again, it's hard to say. These pirates are starting to all look alike. He asked for my name and number."

"Of course he did. Did you give them to him?"

"No, silly. I'm not that desperate. He was cute in an enthusiastic adolescent sort of way. I told him I'd probably see him around. That's it." A faint blush made its way up June's neck to her cheeks. She lowered her eyes as Detective Rains scrutinized her long enough to make her squirm.

"When was the last time you remember having it?" Rains asked.

"What?"

"Your wallet. When was the last time you remember having it?"

"Don't you have a murder to solve, Detective Rains? Why do you care so much about a misplaced wallet?"

I was surprised by June's snippy reaction, but I got that she was disappointed, maybe even uncomfortable about his attention. Rains just shrugged and leaned back against the seat, looking like he was in for the long haul. June glanced at him in the rearview mirror and pulled back onto the street in the direction of the Heinemann's Winery and Crystal Cave.

I expected more questions from the back seat, but the detective was acting like a tourist now, enjoying the scenery on the short ride. Maybe he'd been put off by June's reaction to his inquiry about her wallet, but that was silly. He was a professional. This was his job.

We headed southwest on Catawba Avenue, passing the Chocolate Museum and The Goat Soup and Whiskey Tavern on the way. He asked a few questions, but they were about our experiences on the island, favorite restaurants, and other generic queries about the Lake Erie islands and their history, rather than the murder investigation. Maybe that's what good detectives do—gather intelligence without alerting the suspect. Wait. I wasn't a suspect, at least I hoped I wasn't.

I decided it was time to turn the tables once more. "How long have you lived here, Detective?" I asked. "I get the impression you're not a local."

"Good work, Francie, but seriously, you're right. I've only been in the area since April. I'm still adjusting to the slower pace. I've discovered being on "island time" is a real thing. I have a place on Kelleys Island. I prefer the quieter, less touristy atmosphere there, but I work throughout the whole chain of Lake Erie islands. I'm here on South Bass Island more often than the other islands because of the population. I've learned quickly that Put-in-Bay is a mecca for fun seekers, and that fun often includes consuming too much alcohol and doing things most people regret in the morning, or when they get picked up by the cops."

I laughed at his accurate assessment and added, "That's why we almost always come in the middle of the week. I can't even remember the last time I've been inside the Beer Barrel or the Roundhouse."

"Those two establishments do get more than their fair share of trouble. Most of it is minor stuff the beat cops can handle, but once in a while I get called over to sort things out. I'm as busy as I care to be, and it's a far cry from Chicago."

"Chicago? What's with you detectives and Chicago? Jack is from Chicago too. He moved out here in January. Did you know him when you were there? Did he convince you to move? Do you know anything about the case he's currently testifying in?" I was getting pretty good at this interrogation thing. At least the part about asking questions. Not so much learning the answers to my questions.

We had arrived at our destination. Satisfying my curiosity about Lucas Rains's past was going to have to wait. June parked in front of the winery and switched off the ignition. Rains stepped out of the cart, walked around to the passenger side, and extended a hand to help me down. So, he was a gentleman in addition to a misplaced city dweller. I would have enjoyed learning a little more about this interesting man. I suspected my friend shared my feelings and then some. A chirp from June's back pocket diverted her attention, and she stayed in her seat to answer the call.

Rains waited a moment, but when it was evident June wasn't ending her conversation with the caller, he decided not to hang around. "I'll talk to you ladies inside. Thanks for the ride."

"Well, that was different." I walked around to the driver's side and caught the tail end of June's conversation. "Was that Jack? Was it something important?" I asked.

"Yes, it was important. No it wasn't Jack. It was my editor." June looked around making sure there were no inquisitive eyes or ears attached to anyone lurking about before she continued. "She was just checking on my progress with the pirate article, but when I informed her we stumbled into a murder investigation last night, she got really excited. Francie, this could be my golden ticket. If I can get to the bottom of Truffle's murder before the cops and be the first one to break the story, I could make some serious cash. Will you help me?"

"Will I help you? Is the pope Catholic? Does a bear...never mind. Of course I'll help you! You know I used to want to work in criminal investigation. I've even taken a class or two when I could fit it in under professional development. The range of acceptable courses is pretty broad in the theater department. We can do this. The police have their hands full with the holiday weekend, and Detective Rains never even got around to asking us about Truffle on the ride over."

"In his defense, it was only a half mile ride."

"Maybe we should look for him and pump him for information," I offered.

"Or maybe we should see what we can discover on our own."

"Or that. Let's go inside and get our next clue for the treasure hunt. Then we can decide."

After the bright sunshine outside, the darkness of the room was startling. We stood around shuffling our feet and talking in low tones while our eyes adjusted. When I could take in my surroundings, the first thing I saw was an influx of people entering from the opposite side of the building. One of the day's scheduled tours of Crystal Cave had just ended, and it let out directly into the spacious, brightly lit gift shop. Most of the adults passed on through to the dark space of the bar where we had entered. The children stayed in the shop happily gathering polished rocks, crystals, and other souvenirs from their visit to the world's largest geode, confident their parents would be compelled to purchase the treasures they had selected.

"What are we supposed to do now? If this is where the clue leads, there should be something else to find, or pick up, right?"

"I'm guessing we show our wristbands to prove we got our first clue. The fact we're here proves we figured out the first riddle."

June was pointing at her black wristband. "Maybe these things entitle us to some free samples. Let's start at the bar. Bartenders always know what's going on."

June was right. The plastic sample cups lined up at the end of the bar were meant for the *Angel's Trumpet* treasure hunt participants. As predicted, when the bartender saw our wristbands, she handed me a new envelope. "Good luck to you and have fun. Enjoy your free wine flight and tour."

"We get a free tour of the cave too?" The barkeep smiled at June's childlike enthusiasm. "Nothing like some giant stalactites to get the creative juices flowing."

I thanked the bartender for her help. "Did the other teams pick up their envelopes yet?" I asked offhandedly.

She flashed her smile at me this time. "I can't tell you, but don't stop asking questions. It's the only way you'll ever get the answers you need."

I took her words as a sign, thinking they could be applied to more than just this treasure hunt. I walked away, caught up in my thoughts, inspecting the envelope in my hand. I'm usually good at multitasking—walking, thinking, inspecting—but I guess four things at once was too much to handle. I wasn't looking where I was going.

Oof! I looked up to see who was slowing my progress to the complimentary wine. No surprise, it was Detective Rains.

"Be sure to try the ice wine. It's great on a warm day like today."

I could feel my face heat up as I remembered telling him I had no intention of drinking so early in the day.

"Will you be tagging along with us for the entire afternoon, Detective?" June asked. "Just so you know, I don't intend to share my wine samples, even if you are tall, dark, and handsome."

That comment shut him right up. Obviously June had no guilt about day drinking, or for that matter, flirting. Rains may have won round one in the golf cart, but June had just scored big in round two.

The blush in Lucas Rains's cheeks only enhanced his perfect chocolate mocha skin tone. "I think I'll keep my afternoon open, but I'll be around. Try to stay out of trouble ladies, and enjoy the hunt."

What was that supposed to mean? For being a detective, this guy didn't seem to do much investigating. I sat down at the bar and looked over the selections lined up in plastic cups ranging from a dry red to the vineyard's famous sweet ice wine. I chose a red blend from the middle of the line-up. June sat next to me and selected the ice wine.

"Here's to winning this treasure hunt!" June raised her sample cup toward me.

"And finding out who killed poor Chef Truffle," I whispered.

June replied in a hushed tone to match mine. "What do you think Rains is up to? He never did ask us anything. And why is he telling us to stay out of trouble?"

"I think it's highly probable Jack filled Rains in on our last two holiday weekends. And now this. Seriously. Do you know anyone else who can say they've added murder investigations to three out of three of their recent vacations? Since I'm the one who stumbled across the chef's body, literally, I'm sure he thinks he needs to keep an eye on us—either to protect us or see if we lead him to the murderer. It bothers me, you know. If the killer knows we were there in the galley, he might think we know more than we should. He could be after us next."

"We need to keep our guard up, for sure. I don't like the idea of being bait."

We stopped talking when Bradley sauntered over and leaned against the bar next to June's stool. Or was it Zach? Why couldn't I keep their names straight? They looked nothing alike, their personalities were completely different, and I am the mother of twins myself. I was familiar with the phenomenon, but never thought it would apply to me.

"What's going on over here, ladies? I figured you'd both be chomping at the bit to figure out the next clue. I'm rather bored myself. I might just go back to the ship."

"Really, Zach?" June cozied up a little closer to him. "I thought you were all gung-ho about the itinerary and getting a head start on the competition. Now you're bored. What changed your mind?"

"Um, what are you talking about? I was never that excited about this scavenger hunt, and by the way, it's Bradley." For whatever reason, June was having the same trouble telling the brothers apart as I was.

I decided to change the direction of the talk away from the treasure hunt to something neutral. Trivia usually did the trick, and I'd collected enough island trivia over the last few months. I might as well share it.

"Aren't you at least going to get your free wine samples and take the cave tour? I figured you and your brother, of all people, would be interested in the tour."

I saw a spark of interest in his eyes. "Oh yeah, why's that?"

"Because you're the experts on island history, aren't you? Did you know Crystal Cave was discovered in 1897 by workers digging a well for the winery? Since it was on the property, the Heinemanns also owned the full rights to the cave. Crystal Cave helped save the family-run winery during Prohibition. Tours of the cave helped pay the bills while other wineries on the island were forced to close their doors."

Bradley wasn't biting. "My brother's research focus is pirates on the Great Lakes, not business diversity in the twenties. As fascinating as your story is, I've heard it all before." He paused a moment before adding, "I think I'll order a cheese plate and go outside. Feel free to join me when you finish with your history lesson." He turned and strode out the door.

June was staring after our shipmate. "What's gotten into everyone? He was super friendly during dinner, and I enjoyed dancing with him. I hope he isn't going to ruin the fun of this treasure hunt by acting all superior just because he already knows all the island history."

"Wait. Did he say cheese plate? Maybe he isn't so bad after all. You know, June, I could use a snack. We're going to have to be creative about meals until we figure out how to get access to our bank accounts again. Let's go help him with that cheese plate."

June offered me her brightest smile. "I like how you think. We can't conduct a murder investigation on an empty stomach."

When we stepped out the back door into the winery's yard to look for Bradley and the cheese, I had to grab June's arm and stop short to avoid another collision. The Fullers rushed past us, not stopping to say hello. Marla was all excited about the free cave tour and was trying unsuccessfully to impart her enthusiasm to her offspring. Liz was looking past her mother through the door to the bar where the free wine samples were. It was evident what she would have preferred to do. I thought about what it would be like having to drag Beth along with me, but I suspected we would have made the best of it and found a way to have a good time since we actually enjoyed each other's company. Oh well, Marla and Liz were not my problem.

Zach approached the mother-daughter duo with outstretched arms and a wide smile, "Ladies, would you both like to join me in the free cave tour? I've never been, and it sounds pretty amazing."

What was amazing was how Liz had a sudden change of heart and skipped off happily with Zach toward the tour guide manning the cave entrance. Marla scrambled to keep pace, and I couldn't tell if she was happy or miffed about the whole thing, but again, not my problem.

We chose a table in the middle of the garden where we could see people coming or going from any direction. I didn't see Bradley or his cheese plate anywhere.

June sat with her back to the tabletop, her ballerina legs stretched out on the grass in front of her. June wasn't really a ballerina, but you wouldn't know by looking at her. Her petite frame was anything but fragile. She could just as easily be a gymnast or a stealth ninja with a flair for hair. I used to think she color-dyed her hair streaks to coordinate with her outfits, but I recently figured out she had a large collection of clip-in hairpieces to expedite her creative quick changes.

I looked around the garden as I sipped my free wine. I still had the unopened envelope from the bartender but decided to put off opening it until June was ready to look at its contents with me. The grounds were filling up fast with interesting folks. One of my favorite things to do in public places has always been people watching. While I tried to imagine lives, families, and jobs to go along with all the characters, June concentrated on the screen of her cell phone. I gave her a few more minutes before breaking the silence. "So, Ms. Reporter, what's our plan?"

She tucked her phone back into her pocket and turned her attention to me. "I think for now, we need to stick to the script and participate in the treasure hunt. We should keep our eyes and ears open and look for chances to learn everything about everyone staying on the *Angel's Trumpet.*"

Chapter 7

"I was talking about our plan to score some snacks, but your plan is good too. Did you find something interesting on your phone? Where should we start?"

"Let's start with the victim." June retrieved her lifeline from her pocket yet again. I was going to have to invent a system for wearing a cell phone as a fashion accessory. I'd make millions, and think of all the worn pockets I'd rescue.

"Look what popped up when I put Chef Truffle's name in my advanced search engine." June scrolled through her phone to the spot she wanted and handed it to me.

"Theodore? How did you know his first name was Theodore?"

"Give me some credit here. I'm a snoop who gets the scoop."

"Seriously, June?"

"Okay, but it's true. I saw it in Detective Rains's notebook when he was questioning us in the galley. I remembered it. Who wouldn't?"

I skimmed over the article on the screen. "What's this about the Hotel Victory? I never heard of it."

"Keep reading. I didn't know anything about it either, and that alone baffles me. For all the times we've been on South Bass Island, you'd have thought we would both be well aware of its history."

Now my curiosity was piqued. I started back at the beginning and took my time. When I was finished, I had much to consider. "First of all, I can't believe I didn't know about the hotel. For crying out loud, the biggest hotel in the United States, and maybe even the world at that time? I've spent months entrenched in island history, but I suppose not many pirates booked rooms there. Seriously, June?"

She ran her fingers through her hair. "You said that already. Yep. There were six hundred sixty guest rooms—that's twice as many rooms as the Grand Hotel on Mackinac Island. And to top it off, it went out in a blaze of glory in 1919. People reported seeing the smoke and flames from as far away as Sandusky and even Detroit."

"So what does this have to do with Truffle?" I turned back to the article looking for a reference.

"I'm not sure if it means anything, but it turns out his great grandmother, Hazel Henry, was an employee of the Hotel Victory from 1899 until August, 1919, when it burned down. This same Ms. Henry was interviewed by several publications since she was one of only a few eye-witnesses willing to share her story."

"I still don't get the connection. Why would anyone be interested in where the chef's great grandmother was employed, or for that matter, commit murder as a result? Lots of people have long-standing ties to the islands and family histories dotted with scandal and tragedy."

"I'm still working on that. She's one of the people who went through the guest rooms after the fire and helped retrieve and catalog belongings that weren't carried off by looters." June reached over and took her phone back. "Here it is." She found the place she was looking for and handed it back to me. "See the reference to something she found in one of the premier rooms? I need more time, but it sounds like she could have stumbled across some items belonging to a woman of some renown."

"As in someone who may have possessed something of great value?" The wheels in my brain spun into gear.

As I tried to connect the dots, I looked out across the green lawn, past the picnic tables and horseshoe pits. Cole Blackhart stood alone in the shade of a weeping willow lighting a cigar. Seeing him there was like wavering on the threshold of a time machine with one foot in and one foot out. Blackhart wore civilian clothing. His coal black, wavy hair usually worn loose around his shoulders was tied back in a ponytail, and in place of his leather and ruffles, he sported well-worn jeans and a pressed white shirt open at the collar. Even without his pirate attire, I could imagine him ordering his crew to go ashore during the fire at the Hotel Victory and lay claim to anything of value. I also imagined Rose, my alter ego, or imaginary friend, or whatever she was, would not have been impressed by his good looks.

On the other hand, Blackhart looked perfectly at home in the winery garden relaxing with a good cigar which is exactly what my husband would have been doing if he were here. He would also probably be telling me to mind my own business and stay out of the detective's way, so all things considered, maybe it was a good thing Hamm was still on the mainland for a while. I had to remind myself to stay on track and in the present. We were trying to solve a treasure hunt and a murder on a vacation island, not dig up mysteries from the past.

"Look, June. The captain's here."

"Where? I don't see any pirates."

"No. He's wearing regular clothes. In fact, here he comes." The best-looking man in the winery garden sauntered over to our table.

"Francesca, how nice to see you here. Hello, June. You obviously made your way here by solving your first riddle. Did you pick up your next clue at the bar?"

"Yes. Good to see you too." It was an effort not to stare at his handsome face. "I almost didn't recognize you."

"Oh, well, yes. I can't wear my pirate clothes nonstop. They're not as comfortable as they look."

June laughed at the obvious joke and met Blackhart's intense gaze. Even without his eyeliner, his eyes were mysterious and compelling.

"Have you figured out your clue yet? I see the other guests have already gone."

"As a matter of fact, we were just about to take a look at it." I held up the still-sealed envelope. "Is it cheating for you to sit with us while we open it?"

"Well, no, I suppose not." He slid onto the picnic table bench beside June. She flipped her legs up and around, so she could be facing the table too.

Without breaking eye contact, June spoke sweetly. "Captain, it's awful about Chef Truffle. He was a friend of yours. It must be hard to go about business as usual with such a tragic event weighing on you. Are you any closer to finding out what happened?"

She was doing her job and doing it well. I sat across from the two and kept my mouth shut. For now.

"The police are doing everything they can. I'm trying to keep busy the best way I know how—by keeping my ship and crew operating at peak performance. It wasn't easy getting someone to take over Theo's duties in the galley for the weekend. He had your recipes perfected."

Who did take his place?" I asked with the utmost concern.

"No one you would know, of course." He seemed to be considering how much more to tell us. "I brought in an acquaintance from the mainland."

"You were lucky to find someone available on such short notice," I said.

"And on a holiday weekend," June added.

"The contest sponsors were very helpful. They have a lot at stake here. They invested a good deal of money into putting this whole thing together and will do whatever it takes to make sure there are no more glitches."

Was he for real? Glitches? I hoped being in the wrong place at the wrong time wouldn't end up being a glitch for June or me. I looked at Captain Blackhart with a more critical eye than before. Was his being here really a coincidence, or did he have some other motivation?

"Did the new chef have time to recreate the winning recipes?" I asked. "What did you say his name was?"

"Speaking of winning recipes, look what's on its way over." Blackhart expertly dodged my question. Or maybe I was being paranoid.

I saw waiters with trays heading into the garden. One of them approached our table, and I nearly swooned as the young man placed three red-and-white-checked cardboard baskets overflowing with delicious-smelling chicken wings in front of us.

"Enjoy, folks. This is compliments of the *Angel's Trumpet* and the sponsors of the pirate recipe contest. There are comment cards under the baskets. Please feel free to let the creator of the recipe know how you enjoy the dish."

I forgot all about the cheese plate, the still-sealed envelope, and my questions about the integrity of the captain. The sweet, spicy aroma drifting up to my nose was like a drug. For the next few minutes, the only sounds coming from our table were those of finger licking and sighs of pleasure. Finally, there was nothing left in our checkered baskets but bones and sauce-covered napkins.

"I believe this answers your question about the new chef's ability to prepare the recipes, Francesca." Blackhart smiled as he wiped a bit of jerk sauce from the corner of his mouth. "He's probably working on a batch of your pirate stew for this afternoon. If the wings are any indication, I think you'll be pleased with the result."

I couldn't argue. The wings were delicious, but their sweet, spicy flavor had left me thirsty. I reached for my plastic cup, which was nearly empty, and besides, wine wasn't what I needed to fix the problem.

Blackhart picked up on my thoughts. "Let me get you both some ice water. I could use some myself." He got to his feet, but before he took his leave, he reached down to the grass and picked up the envelope containing our next clue. Handing it to me, he said, "You must have dropped this. It's probably a good thing, though, seeing how everything on the table is covered in sauce."

I took the envelope with my sticky fingers. "Thank you. And thanks for getting water. We'll need some to drink and some to rinse our hands off."

June and I watched Blackhart walk back to the winery to get our drinks. A sleek black cat trotted close beside him, so close he nearly tripped over it more than once. It must have been the same kitty rubbing against my leg and meowing under the picnic table as we devoured our food. Cats were routine visitors in the winery gardens. They roamed about freely and were often treated to bits of cheese and crackers. It was no wonder one had found a prime spot under our table. Blackhart must have spilled some sauce on his pant leg. Whatever the reason, it looked like he had a new best friend.

"We might as well open this while we wait." I tore the side of the envelope and extracted a thin strip of paper. "Hopefully, it'll be an easy clue, and we can figure it out before the captain gets back. Marla and Zach are in the cave meaning either the next clue's down there and they already found it, or they'll be delayed until the tour is over and we can get a head start.

"What does it say?"

I smoothed the paper out and read the printed message slowly. *Glittering points that wandrowd truths/Sparkling spears that veren trus.*

"What is that supposed to mean? It doesn't make any sense."

I passed the paper over to June. "See for yourself. I think the letters are scrambled in some of the words."

I stared at the words on the paper June now held, but nothing came to mind. "What are *wandrowd truths*?" I wondered aloud. "And *veren trus*? I've never come across these words in any of my reading. How about you?"

"Do you think glittering points and sparkling spears have anything to do with stuff in the gift shop? There are lots of sparkly crystals and things in there."

"We could go check it out. Maybe we can discover something. If not, I might pick up some souvenirs for the kids. Ben still has the rocks he started collecting here when he was eight, and Beth wouldn't say no to a pretty crystal pendant."

June wadded up the paper and shoved it in her pocket. "Here comes Blackhart. Let's keep this to ourselves for now."

"Sorry, it took me so long. I had to drink my water and wash up inside. I couldn't carry three glasses without spilling, especially with this cat tripping me up every step I take."

June bent down and scooped up the cat. "She's beautiful. Is she yours? Does she have a name?"

"We've only just met, but you'd think she was my long lost soulmate or something. I can't shake her for the life of me."

"She doesn't have a collar." I stroked her silky fur as she purred on June's lap. "You might as well accept the fact you've been adopted. What will you call her?"

"I'll think about it. Maybe she's just leading me on. I don't want to jump the gun by naming her. In the meantime, you two better think about getting your next clue. I saw your shipmates leaving through the gift shop. They must have found their clues during the cave tour because none of them are sticking around here."

"Great," I said, taking a long draught of ice water. "The next tour isn't for another hour."

Captain Blackhart was still holding the glass of water meant for June. "You better drink this before the ice melts."

She stopped petting her furry friend and reached for the offered refreshment. Without warning, a crazy neon whirlwind swooped down and knocked the full glass out of Blackhart's hand showering June and the cat, neither of whom was impressed. The cat recovered first and decided to make the most of the situation, lapping up the water that had pooled in a dip of the uneven planks of the picnic tabletop.

"What the?" June jumped to her feet. The cat screeched and bounded away. Blackhart apologized.

"It's not your fault, Captain," June reassured him as she shook off her hands. "I think the poor kitty was thirsty. That's probably why she was following you. Pretty Boy, on the other hand, is really getting on my nerves. What's up with that bird?"

"He misses his master, I'm afraid. He hasn't been the same since..."

"I don't know about that," I interrupted. He's acting about the same as the first time I met him, and that was before..." I clamped my mouth shut realizing how callous my remark was and glad I shut up when I had.

To his credit, Blackhart graciously ignored my lapse in manners. "In any case, I'm sorry about the drink."

"It was just water. I'll be dry in no time. Besides, I think we should focus on getting on with our quest. I sure don't want to end up in last place. How are we going to get down into the cave before the next tour?"

Blackhart stroked the shadow of a beard along his strong jawline. "There might be a
way," he said thoughtfully.

Chapter 8

The captain was right. The entrance to the cave was unattended when we got there, and June and I slipped unnoticed through the narrow opening and down the steep rock stairs into the dark, damp cavern beneath the winery. Crystal Cave, the world's largest geode, is a vug, a large cavity within a single rock. Above us and all around us, bluish-green celestite crystals, some almost two feet long, glowed eerily. I imagined this is what it might look like on another planet or maybe a mystical castle in a fantasy novel.

"What's that?" I stopped and pointed to something glinting in the ghostly light just out of my reach.

"Why are you whispering?"

"I don't know. Maybe because we snuck down here, and I'd rather not cause a scene. Could you stop talking for a minute?"

On a shallow ledge about waist-high, stood three silver boxes, about an inch square, each with an etched symbol on its lid. I was closest to them and bent down to scrutinize them before picking one up. June joined me and removed the other two.

I opened mine, squinting in the unnatural light to get a better look. Inside was a thin strip of printed paper nestled in a purple velvet lining. "It's hard to read down here. I think it might be a clue—or at least part of one. It just says, *but never tire at end of day.*"

A horrible racket interrupted our investigation of the possible clue. Was this place haunted? Was Rose back trying to warn me of unseen danger? I was rethinking the sanity of coming down here alone. Rules are made for reasons, and most of the time I follow them.

Howling, screeching, and crashing on the stairs behind us made me plaster myself against the cave wall and hold my breath. Fur and feathers blew past me. I couldn't determine which of the creatures was faring better, but from the looks of things, both Pretty Boy and Blackhart's new feline friend were on some unstoppable mission to destroy one another. My mission was to steer clear of beaks and claws, so I scrunched low to the floor, tucked my chin, and began inching my way back toward the stairs. Something sharp poked me in the ribs. I screamed.

"Settle down, it's just me." June had no idea how relieved I was to hear that. Besides the obvious animal encroachment, I was feeling crowded out by uninvited spirits—friendly, imagined, or otherwise.

"This place isn't big enough for all of us. I'm right behind you. Let's get out of here."

I concentrated on reaching the stairs and getting out of the cave without being slashed or pecked. Makeshift pirates were one thing, but swashbuckling pets were more than I could bear. I didn't even want to think about my tag-along imaginary friend and tried as hard as I could to banish Rose to the far recesses of my mind. If she wasn't here to help me out, I just as soon she didn't distract me. A few more feet and we'd be at our destination.

Blinding strobes cut through the darkness and froze us in place.

"What's going on down here?"

A mildly overweight security guard in his early twenties lumbered down the steep staircase. He stopped at the bottom, caught his breath, and swept his over-powered flashlight around the dim, dark place making the stalactites sparkle and glow above us. In the bouncing light beams, I caught the name on his gold-colored badge identifying him as Thomas. So far, our attempt to get in and out of the cave undetected was not going well.

Thomas didn't look happy to be down here with us. His forehead was glistening, and he was still having trouble regulating his breathing. The steps were steep, but come on. This guy was young. He didn't look like he was used to regular cardio activity. Maybe he should renew his gym membership, at least for the sake of his job.

"What are you two doing down here? The cave is strictly off-limits during restricted times. And what was all the racket? It sounded like a cat fight."

He was closer to the truth than he knew. It dawned on me that the space was now quiet. There was no sign of feline or fowl. Either they were lurking in the shadows, ready to pounce, or there was another way out of the cave.

June stepped up to the plate. "Hi, Thomas. I'm really sorry if we caused trouble. We heard something whining down here and had to find out if we could help. Turns out, you were right about it being a cat—a cat and a parrot chasing each other around and scaring the bejeebers out of us. We were just about to leave when you got here."

"Where are these animals? I'll need to get them out of the cave. It's not safe for them to stay down here."

I couldn't help myself. "You're worried about them? You should be worried about us, and the next group of tourists who'll be coming down here to see crystals only to be mauled by some crazy pets."

"Are you hurt ma'am?"

June waved me away and sidled up to the young guard, batting her long lashes. "The crystals are so much easier to appreciate with no one else around, don't you think, Thomas?"

"Well, yes, but that doesn't make it okay for you to be here. You have to leave now." Thomas was sweating again, but I had to believe it had more to do with his proximity to June than his aerobic shortcomings this time.

"Of course, and thank you for coming down here to protect me and my friend. You're so brave."

I couldn't tell because his face was now turned away from me, but I was willing to bet Thomas was blushing. June hooked her arm around her admirer's elbow and turned toward the stairs. I scanned the entire space but saw no trace of either of the offensive creatures, so I fell in line behind June and the young guard. We had to walk single file up the steep narrow staircase, so when Thomas stopped short, it set off a chain reaction, knocking June into me and causing me to stumble back onto the slippery floor of the cave. At my feet sat a familiar sleek black cat. She raised her paw and gave it a casual lick.

"There you are, Miss Kitty. Did you hurt yourself during your encounter with Pretty Boy? Where is that scoundrel anyway?"

The cat offered no enlightenment, and I really had no desire to find the parrot, so I redirected my attention to the stairwell where June and Thomas stood in total darkness. Something was blocking the light at the top of the stairs.

The something turned out to be the winery manager. He stood at the top of the stairs like a total eclipse of the sun, blocking our exit and any hope of sneaking in and out of the cave undetected.

"I demand to know what this is all about. Thomas, come up here, and bring the trespassers. I'm calling the police."

Wait. What? This was the opposite of what we were going for. There was no more time for finesse or flirting. Action was required. I did my best impression of my favorite Green Bay linebacker—head first and figure the rest out later. I rammed into June who was forced to push the security guard into the unsuspecting manager who stumbled back into the gift shop. Before he could get his bearings, I shoved my way to the front of the line, shot straight through the brightly-lit shop, and kept on going, through the exit door and out into the afternoon sun with my best friend right behind me.

"Come back here now! Thomas, why are you still here? Go after them!"

That's the last thing I heard because we were running full tilt to the parking lot.

"What are we waiting for, June? Let's get the heck out of here before your new boyfriend catches up."

"I can't find the golf cart key. I must have dropped it." She inspected her elbow. "You could have warned me you were starting a conga line. I whacked my elbow on the wall."

"I'm sorry. There wasn't time, and it would have ruined the element of surprise. Are you okay?"

"No worries. Except we obviously can't go back for the key. Any bright ideas?"

I had expended my brilliance on our exit strategy. "I got nothing," I said, scanning the lot and the street for security or cops. So far, Thomas hadn't reappeared, and I didn't hear any sirens or see flashing lights approaching. There was, however, an intriguing passenger in the golf cart parked next to ours.

June lost no time hopping into the cart and throwing her arms around the neck of the handsome fellow, who, by the way, was a German shepherd. Pacing on the lawn nearby was an intimidating-looking man deep in a phone call. I couldn't have been happier to see either the dog or the man. June looked up and followed my line of sight. She nodded in Michael's direction before turning her attention back to the dog.

"What's going on?" I asked no one in particular. "What are you guys doing here? I asked Gunner, the German shepherd. He cocked his head and raised his paw. It was vague, but it was something.

"Is she flirting with you too, Gunner?"

At the sound of his name, the dog nuzzled June's neck, and she reciprocated by stroking his glossy coat. I heartily approved of this relationship.

The man on the lawn was Michael. Neither of us knew his last name even though he and Gunner played key roles in saving both our tushies not once, but twice this summer. June first made his acquaintance the previous year between writing gigs when she pursued him for an entire month until he agreed to sit with her for an informal interview. Before then, not even the locals knew much about the mysterious pair who went quietly about their business.

June respected his wishes and never printed her feature story on him or even published an editorial. What we knew for sure was he was ex-military and had lots of connections in law enforcement. He loves the laid-back atmosphere of the islands, but reads five newspapers a day from front to back. We never learned enough about his past to explain the haunted look that came over him when he thought no one was watching.

Even from a distance, he gave off a solitary vibe—not exactly menacing—I no longer suspected him of being a killer, but his invisible force field said *keep your distance* loud and clear.

Even sweet, affectionate Gunner was not to be underestimated. He was highly trained and ferociously loyal.

Without warning, June hopped out of the golf cart and headed straight for Michael, leaving me to make small talk with Gunner. He sniffed my hand and pronounced me satisfactory in spite of any essence of cat or parrot lingering about me.

June came back with Michael in tow. Obviously, she had the secret password to unlock his friendship because Michael's gait was easy, and his smile was genuine. At the moment, there was nothing intimidating about the guy, except maybe his good looks.

"Michael's agreed to drive us to the café for the meet and greet," June informed me. I checked my watch and was stunned to see it was nearly time for me to be at my first official public appearance. I was sure I would be automatically disqualified for my chance of becoming the new spokesperson for Paradise Rum if I was a no show. What would be the point of winning the treasure hunt if I couldn't even keep an appointment?

"I could hug you right now," I replied. Leave it to June to be on top of my itinerary in spite of all the interruptions and complications.

The sponsors had arranged for the recipe contest winners to gather at the Old Forge Café this afternoon to meet with the public, showcase our winning creations, and plug our common secret ingredient—Paradise Rum. There was sure to be good attendance. It was being advertised all over town with the keywords *free samples* highlighted in large bold print. And thanks to June, I would actually be there on time to participate.

Michael spoke to me, and his voice was every bit as sexy as I had remembered. "We can stop by the rental place and get a new key for the golf cart, or they can pick it up and bring it to you at your next stop. You know all the keys fit all the ignitions. Some security, huh?"

"Well, thank you, Michael. It's so good to see you, even if the circumstances are less than ideal." He smiled at that. At least a lost golf cart key was better than escaping the jaws of death despite terrible odds.

June slid onto the front seat next to Michael, and I climbed up next to Gunner in the back, happy to share a little love with an animal I knew felt no secret desire to bring about my demise. Michael wasn't much for small talk, so to pass the time, June pulled the two silver boxes from her pocket and began inspecting them. I retrieved the one I had and did likewise.

After scrutinizing the etchings on their lids, she opened one and pulled a slip of paper from inside.

"We retire."

"Huh?"

"That's all it says—the paper in the box. What kind of clue is that?"

"Hmm." I opened my box and found a similar strip of paper. "The one I have says, *but never tire at end of day.* You better look in the third box. I'm guessing they all go together."

"We wave all day."

"Wow, I don't know. Maybe we need to figure out our other clue first. They might be sequential."

"Maybe." June turned to Michael. "Do you know what *wandrowd truths* are? Is it a legal term? Have you ever heard anyone say that?"

"What kind of truths?" he asked. June spelled it out for him.

"What does the rest of the clue say?"

June recited the whole thing to him from memory.

"No, no. Not truths, thrust."

That got my attention. "Huh? What are you talking about?"

"The word is not truths; it's thrust. Some of the words in your clue are scrambled. Look at it again."

I still had the paper with the clue we picked up from the bartender. I held it up so June could reread it with me. *Glittering points that wandrowd truths/Sparkling spears that veren trus.*

Then it hit me. "Stalactites! It's talking about the stalactites in the cave. It makes perfect sense. That's why they gave us free tours—so we'd find the silver clue boxes. *Glittering points that downward thrust/Sparkling spears that never rust.* It seems so obvious."

Michael's lips were turned up at the corners, but he said nothing. June sighed and said, "Yes, you're right about everything. It doesn't matter now, though. We found the next clues without using the last one. It was Captain Blackhart who pointed us to the cave. I guess we should thank him next time we see him."

Michael's smile disappeared. "Cole Blackhart sent you down into the cave without a guide?"

"Yes he did," June replied. "He helped us get to our next clue, so we wouldn't fall behind the other two groups. I thought that was nice of him."

I didn't add the part about the crazy animals or the ineffective security guard, and I sure didn't say anything about the winery manager who threatened to call the cops on us.

Michael said something under his breath. I didn't catch it, but it wasn't a compliment about using our resources.

The short trip to the Old Forge Café didn't allow us time to talk, and there wasn't much to see along the way except the police station on the left and the grocery store on the right. The quaint creperie was situated between the Irish pub and a specialty burger joint. The rest of the storefronts on both sides of the street were either eating and drinking establishments or gift shops showcasing colorful summer-themed wares.

We made it to our destination with a few minutes to spare. Michael dropped us off at the curb without so much as a goodbye. I was grateful for the ride, but I found our driver's behavior unsettling. As he drove off, I waved to Gunner who reciprocated with a thump of his tail. At least he had some social skills. I knew from experience Michael had our backs one hundred percent, but his demeanor still threw me, and I wondered once more what secrets he kept.

Marla, Liz, and Zach were already there. Bradley was approaching on foot. He had to park their golf cart a block away and walk back, which explained why Michael had done what he did. It was simple logistics, but still, he could have said goodbye.

Chapter 9

There was a long table set up just inside the low wrought iron fence in front of the red brick building. Only three chairs were positioned behind the table, making it evident it would be just the recipe contest winners seated in this area. Our guests and friends would have to sit at the tables scattered about the front and side yards.

"I guess I'll talk to you later, June. Looks like it's time to earn my perks."

"Enjoy the spotlight. I'll go mingle with the common folk." She skipped away to find a good spot to people-watch while enjoying her free food. So far, we'd both managed to stay well-fed considering neither of us had any buying power to speak of.

I pulled out the end chair closest to me and sat down, happy when Zach chose the chair in the middle. I'd get a chance to talk to him, and I wouldn't have to make small talk with Marla who was settling herself in the chair on the other side of Zach. It was time to put on my best celebrity smile and throw myself into the task of chatting with the people who stopped by.

As promised, there were free samples of my pirate stew, Zach's jerk chicken wings, and Marla's Triple-X rum cake for the visitors to sample. Unfortunately, the spread was laid out on the other side of the courtyard. The only things on our table were three pitchers of raspberry lemonade and stacks of each of our recipe cards. I could hear people raving about the delicious food. I knew my stew was good; I had eaten my fill of the wings at the winery; but now I had a serious craving for cake and needed to get some right away.

"Excuse me for a moment. I have to visit the restroom. I promise I won't be gone long." It was lame but it was the only thing I could come up with while I had cake on my mind.

I got up and made a beeline for the buffet table. I'd been anticipating my second slice of Marla's dessert, and when the smiling pirate in charge of food service handed me one, I nearly swooned. The forkful of fragrant cake was just about to reach my lips when it was plucked away and popped straight into Hamm's pie hole.

I was stunned to see my husband. "What are you doing here, Hamm? You said you wouldn't be able to make it until tonight. I'm so happy to see you."

"Oh, man, I can't believe how good this cake is." I could barely make out the words with his mouth crammed full of my food. "Isn't this the best thing you ever tasted?"

I punched my dear husband in the arm. "I wouldn't know," I said, swiping back my fork in the hopes of salvaging a morsel. Now I wished I hadn't stuck almost the entire piece on my fork. "Thanks to you, I didn't even get a taste." I looked at the pathetic crumbs on the paper plate in my hand. They weren't worth trying to collect, so I tossed it all in a nearby trash can.

Hamm tried to look contrite. "If it makes you feel better, people are all raving about your stew. Look at this place. It's obvious this event is drawing a lot of customers to the café. You're stimulating the economy. Come to think of it, you're stim...Ouch! Quit punching me."

"Well, thanks for a whole lot of nothing. Now I have to go back to my post and starve." I was so happy Hamm was back I couldn't stay mad. "I missed you. Walk with me and fill me in on what's going on at the marina and June's boat. Is it fixed? Have you seen June yet?"

Hamm put his arm around my shoulder and pulled me close. "Sorry about the cake. It was really good though." I gave him one last half-hearted punch with my free hand and matched my stride to his. He kept his arm around me as we walked back to my empty seat at the recipe winner's table.

"The marina is finally clear of contamination, so at least people can get back to using their boats. The weekend won't be a total wash. Unfortunately, there's not much to report about June's boat. I left Beacon Pointe after I talked to the repair guy on the phone for the third time. It's a holiday weekend, and you know how that is."

I did. People around here moved to the tick of a different clock. It was part of what made the islands so relaxing and fun, except when your city brain wanted something done. Throw a long weekend in, and you might as well forget appointments, schedules or timelines.

"The boat's not going to sink. It's out of the water for now, and I called in a favor from a friend in the insurance business. Someone's there estimating the cost, so when a repair person is available, he won't have to wait for authorization."

What he wasn't saying but I knew he was thinking was he wanted June's boat back in its slip as soon as possible so we wouldn't have to invite her to stay with us when we got back. Not that she would. She was independent, had lots of friends and resources, and most of all, she was not a mooch. My two favorite people in the world sometimes behaved irrationally when they spent too much time together, but in the end, we all made it work.

Hamm and I were standing in front of the table, and I could feel Marla's disapproving stare boring into my back. It was time to sit down and get back to business. I gave Hamm's hand a final squeeze and returned to my station.

"Thanks so much for taking care of everything. Did I tell you how glad I am that you're here?"

He bent over the table and gave me a sweet peck on the cheek. "Go knock 'em dead with your stew, Francie. Speaking of food, I think I'll grab a bowl and find a seat."

"What? You went for the cake before you tried my stew?" I put on my best air of disbelief and disappointment, but he wasn't buying it.

"You know what they say about life being uncertain. You've got to eat dessert first. Besides, I had insider access to your stew. I already know how delicious it is." He kissed my other cheek as atonement for his sins. "I see an empty chair under a tree with my name on it. I think I can smoke a cigar out here, and if not, I'm sure I can find something to amuse me while you do your celebrity thing."

I spotted June sitting at a café table with Bradley and Liz. She appeared to be enjoying the heck out of a bowl of my pirate stew. Sadly for her, she couldn't indulge in the Triple-X rum cake since one of the ingredients in Marla's winning dessert was chocolate. There wasn't much, but she couldn't risk having an allergic reaction. I felt her pain. I squirmed in my seat trying to get comfortable on the hard plastic chair, deciding to take my mind off my own dietary misfortune by striking up a conversation with Zach.

I had to wait my turn to speak with my colleague while a group of scantily-clad young women plied him with questions about his jerk wings recipe as well as some non-food related queries. He smiled graciously, answering all their questions and engaging them in witty banter. I was about to concede failure to the groupies, when a white-haired gentleman broke through the cluster of cuties and greeted Zach.

"Hello Mr. Zach. It's great to see you back! How are you? I didn't know you would be returning to the island so soon. You're sitting on the winner's side of that table, meaning one of those great dishes came from your kitchen. Let me guess. It's the wings. Am I right?"

Zach didn't reply. His face was getting blotchy. I wondered if he was having an allergic episode, which caused me to lament my lost purse yet again. I always carried a spare EpiPen, but without my bag, I could be of no service.

"If you need a ride back to where you're staying," the visitor broke the awkward silence, "just give me a ring. I'm sure you still have my number. My cab is running till two a.m. all weekend. I'll take care of you." He swept his hand out indicating the rest of our party. "Your friends too. Pervis at your service." The man, Pervis I assumed, bowed from the waist, turned on his heels, and strode off toward a green taxi van emblazoned with his company's slogan, "Pervis at Your Service." Zach still hadn't spoken.

After witnessing the odd encounter between Zach and the taxi driver, I decided I wasn't in the mood to coax a conversation out of an unwilling partner, so I checked my watch and settled in for some serious people watching. I noticed Pervis had walked past his van and was now holding court at the food and drink station. Hamm circled the table, perhaps scouting for an overlooked slice of cake to present to me as a peace offering, but when he concluded there was none to be had, he joined Detective Rains who was seated alone next to the table occupied by June, Bradley, and Liz. I presumed he chose the spot not because it was next to June, but because Rains was rolling an unlit cigar between his fingers. He may have found a smoking buddy. If I leaned forward and strained my ears, I could make out some of the conversations coming from the vicinity of Hamm and the rest of the group.

"I don't know what you want me to say, Detective." June's voice was higher-pitched than usual and carried across the lawn loud and clear.

Rains put his cigar back in his pocket and pulled out his notebook. He flipped through it, found the spot he wanted, and picked up his conversation with June. I couldn't hear what he was saying, but whatever it was, it had my friend all riled up.

"We've been over this. I don't know anything more than I told you last time. Neither Francie nor I had ever seen Truffle before. She just wanted a doggie bag for...Hamm! You're here!"

I smiled from my vantage point seeing June's reaction to finding Hamm standing close enough to reach out and touch her. She popped out of her seat and hugged my hubby. Detective Rains looked on quizzically.

"Hi, June. It's nice to see you too."

She released Hamm from her powerful grip and stepped back. "Sorry, you took me by surprise. Hey, everyone, this is Hammond Egge, Francie's husband. Hamm, this is everyone. I mean, meet Bradley, Liz, and Detective Lucas Rains. She ticked off the names, nodding at each as she did.

"Hi, Mr. Egge," Liz said with a lack of enthusiasm worthy of a prize. I gave her credit, though—when she noticed Hamm's total lack of recognition, she offered him a point of reference. "I'm Liz Fuller. I'm on Beth's swim team at State. I'm here with my mom, Marla. She won a prize for her cake."

"Nice to meet you, Liz. I know the swim team is here on a trip and my daughter has been looking forward to it for some time. You must be very proud of your mom to give that up and hang out with her instead."

Here's where I had to count on my best friend to take care of what I wasn't in a position to do. She did not disappoint. June elbowed Hamm sharply in the ribs.

"Ow. Oh, the cake. That was some cake. I'll have to be sure to thank your mother. Well, have fun."

Good save, Hamm. I was enjoying this rare opportunity to be a fly on the wall. I felt a twinge of guilt as Hamm rubbed his side. He'd endured more than his usual allotment of pokes and punches from the opposite sex today. Rains extended his hand in greeting and introduced himself again, leaving out the sarcastic tone June had used when she said his name.

"Nice to meet you." Hamm returned the handshake. "I should thank you, Detective. I felt terrible that I wasn't there with Francie when she and June found the chef. She must have been terrified. She had every right to be scared, and I'd have given anything to have been there for her."

"She handled the whole ordeal remarkably well. To be honest, I was a little surprised at how calm both ladies were considering the circumstances; and please, call me Lucas."

Now I got why June was upset. She didn't want to be perceived as a helpless female, breaking under a stressful situation. For that matter, neither did I. Did the fact we were helpful and articulate make us appear guilty to the detective? We both wanted nothing more than to see Truffle's killer brought to justice. Why couldn't we all just get along?

Either June was tired of sitting and had had her fill of food, or she was still irritated by Rains's remarks because she got up and left without so much as a see you later to Hamm or the others. Hamm called after her. "June, about your boat."

She didn't pause or even acknowledge him. What was that all about? I thought she'd want to hear the news.

I was distracted by June's actions and missed the rest of the conversation. Hamm and Lucas were talking like old friends, and both of them were now holding unlit cigars.

June crossed the street, power-walked to the corner, turned, and retraced her route. She nearly ran into Pervis's green taxi while dodging golf carts, and stopped to have a few words with him before returning to my table.

"Hey, Francie, it's about time to wrap it up here. The food's almost gone. There's some good lemonade though if you're thirsty." She noticed Zach scratching at the blotches on his neck. "You look thirsty, Zach. In fact, you look like you're about to have a heat stroke. Pervis, over there, was just talking about you. Says you've been a regular on the island over the last few months. Says you're quite the researcher. Funny. I thought it was your brother who was the research guy."

Zach got to his feet so abruptly he tipped his chair over. "What do you know? You don't know anything about me or my brother. Heck, you can't even keep our names straight." He stalked across the road, pulling at his collar and glancing over his shoulder at the taillights of a cop car driving by at a snail's pace.

"What's eating him?" June asked. "I was just trying to make conversation. Maybe if I knew more about him, I'd be able to remember his name."

"I have no clue. He started getting weird when Pervis the cabbie brought up his recent visits to the island. I never got the chance to get the real scoop. I was under the impression this was Zach's first trip to Put-in-Bay. He said as much earlier today. Or had it been Bradley who mentioned it. Honestly, I can't keep those brothers straight either. I'm afraid I'm going to call them by the wrong name every time I talk to them. I know twins can be really touchy about it, and I don't blame them. It's an identity thing. I'm thankful my kids don't have to worry about that issue. They have the twin bond, but people don't have trouble remembering who's who."

June chuckled. "I guess I get the identity thing. Being called the wrong name all the time would get old. What I don't get, though, is why he overreacted to the question about the research. What's the big deal? Who even cares? Unless, of course, he's trying to hide something."

I agreed with June and decided it was time to move on to more important things. "I think I'll take you up on that lemonade before it's all gone. Maybe Bradley has some idea why Zach is behaving so strangely." I pushed my chair up to the table nice and tidy, waved goodbye to Marla who was staring into space, and officially ended my stint at the meet and greet.

"Let's go get Hamm and get some of that lemonade before we take him to the ship. I can't wait to see his face when he gets on board. Isn't it great he finally made it to the island? I was so excited to see him, and I'm sure you were happy to hear the latest news about your houseboat." I threw in the latter comment to see how she'd respond.

"Wow. I guess I was kind of an ass back there. You heard?" I nodded.

"I appreciate everything Hamm's done, and I'll be sure to thank him properly. It's just that detective—he got me all worked up."

"I noticed. He is awfully handsome. What is that, three men so far this weekend? Oh, wait, make that four. Do we count the security guard? What about the pirate at the inn? How do you keep track? Better yet, how do you choose?"

"They are all easy on the eyes, aren't they?" She smiled wistfully. "They all have very specific agendas too. Sometimes I envy you and Hamm, you know."

I grabbed my friend's hand and gave it a squeeze. Now wasn't the time for bare-your-soul girl talk. "Let's go!"

"I'll meet you there. Why don't you get Hamm. By the time you guys get there, I'll think of something nice to say to him. Besides, I don't feel like seeing Detective Rains right now."

I didn't argue. Best friends know when to cajole and when to back off.

Hamm and I made it to the refreshments seconds too late to get in on the last toast. I felt the urge to cry at the sight of the empty pitcher.

"Who's that guy?" Hamm diverted my attention. "He looks like Johnny Depp, or Captain Sparrow, only bigger and more pirate-y, if that's possible."

Captain Blackhart was holding court, speaking with his arms moving in grand sweeping gestures, showcasing the ruffles, silver, and leather accessories that I'd come to recognize.

"Come on. It's time you met the captain of the *Angel's Trumpet*."

Chapter 10

Captain Blackhart cut his demonstrative conversation short and directed his full attention toward me. I must admit, I felt special when he extended his bejeweled hand and greeted us.

"Francesca, this must be your husband." He and Hamm exchanged a vigorous handshake.

"I'm so glad you could join us. I know it means a lot to your wife that you're here. She's been a real trooper through some difficult times."

We engaged in some pleasantries, mostly nautical talk between the two men, and after a few minutes, my attention wandered back to the missed promise of lemonade. I must have sighed aloud because Blackhart noticed.

"My apologies, Francesca. I'm sure you could use a nice cold drink after sitting in the sun talking to all the visitors. Your recipe is very popular in spite of the heat. I think the kitchen ran out before the event was officially over."

"Since you mention it, I am pretty thirsty."

"There's a fresh batch of lemonade just inside the café, and I brought along a little something to add some pizzazz to the party." He winked at me, nodded at Hamm, and went inside to fetch the reinforcements.

My mood brightened considerably. I took a long, sweet swallow of the ice-cold lemonade Captain Blackhart delivered. As promised, it had a pleasant zing to it.

"I'll take another, please," I said, draining the last drops from the bottom of my glass. "This is delicious. I didn't realize how thirsty I was." Blackhart obliged and refilled my empty glass.

"Hey, girlfriend," June joined us with her own empty glass. "Save some for someone else. There are other thirsty people here, you know."

I conceded. "Sorry. It just seems like I keep missing out on the goodies." I sipped on my refill and willed myself to slow down and enjoy the moment.

"I don't mean to put a damper on the party, but I'd like to stow my bag and get a look at the ship now that the captain has told me all about her. He said I was even welcome on the bridge."

"Uh, oh. You have that glazed look in your eyes. Come on, June. Let's get Hamm to the ship, so he can make up for lost time."

"Sounds like a plan. And Hamm, I'm sorry I was rude to you earlier. I really do appreciate you looking after my houseboat."

I'm sure Hamm was grateful for the apology, but he wasn't used to the role of magnanimous friend. He and June had their love/hate relationship down pat. He looked uncomfortable. He nodded, cleared his throat, and immediately changed the subject. "Where's your golf cart?" Hamm inquired. "I lugged this bag from the ferry to here. I'd rather not have to drag it back to the dock."

"We have a lot to tell you, so I might as well start with the golf cart."

Hamm took the news in stride, and I updated him on everything that had happened since yesterday as we walked to the slip at the public dock where the majestic *Angel's Trumpet* was moored. He laughed out loud when I recounted my several encounters with Pretty Boy. Then he expressed concern and apologized again for not being with me through the ordeal of finding poor Chef Truffle's body, and finally, he congratulated me on the success of my winning recipe and for making good progress on the treasure hunt clues.

"Speaking of the clues," I showed Hamm the silver box I found in the cave. We stopped on the sidewalk as I extracted the slip nestled inside the container. "You're good at riddles. Maybe you can make sense of this."

June chimed in, producing her two boxes and completing the set. "We haven't had a chance to do anything with these yet. Do you want to take a quick break and see if we can figure this out together?"

Hamm gladly plopped down on the nearest bench. There were at least a dozen of them spaced evenly along the sidewalk in front of the marina, so people could relax and enjoy the beautiful view. "Sounds good. My bag is getting heavy, and it's pretty hot. Can I have a look at those?"

I sat next to my husband, breathing in his familiar smell, which always reminded me of fresh cut grass with a hint of patchouli. June paced on the lawn behind our bench bouncing ideas around like ping pong balls in a plastic room. After several tries, we agreed on the proper order of our clues and placed the slips of paper end-to end to form the complete riddle.

We wave all day but never tire. At end of day we retire.

"So what retiree waves all day and isn't tired when the day's over? Maybe it's leading to a senior center?" It seemed improbable, but I was thinking out loud.

"There's no senior center on the island," June said after confirming with Google. "Sounds like a Walmart greeter to me."

Hamm gave her a look. "There's no Walmart here either, and you don't need to check the Internet for that fact."

"Of course!" I exclaimed. I was three for three on the clue-solving board. June and Hamm waited expectantly for me to enlighten them.

"It's a flag. More precisely it's three flags. Three clue boxes, three pieces to the puzzle, three flags waving in front of the Perry Victory Monument. Our next stop is the monument."

The monument was such a central landmark on the island, its precise components didn't register right away. Kind of like the golden arches. You knew they were there, but you didn't stop to consider their meaning every time you passed a McDonald's.

"I'm impressed, Francie." Hamm cocked his head to the right and nodded. It was a gesture I had come to recognize over the years. He was reviewing the facts and drawing a conclusion. When he had it all straight in his mind, he stood and reached for my hand, helping me up. It was time to get to the ship.

"We need to get our golf cart back before we can get back to the treasure hunt," June reminded me.

"You're right. After we drop Hamm's bag off, we can walk over to the rental place. I hope losing the key doesn't turn out to be a big deal."

Hamm chimed in. "It's a lot better than having the key and losing the cart." He reminded me of the incident last time we were on the island. We had parked in the designated lot at the marina we were visiting, but when we were ready to drive to breakfast in the morning, the golf cart was gone. That was when we learned about all the keys fitting all the ignitions. Another boater had mistakenly driven off with our transportation. After reporting the disappearance to the police and the rental agency and riding our bikes all over the island looking for it, we returned to find it parked three spaces from where we had left it.

"Thanks, Hamm. You're right. We know where it is. Someone at the rental will have to drive us to the winery to retrieve it, that's all. Or we could call Pervis. He seemed like a nice guy, and maybe he could tell us something more about Zach's recent visits."

"Who's Pervis, and what are you poking your nose into now?"

Oops. I probably should have kept that idea to myself. I gave Hamm a quick recap of the cab driver and Zach's reaction to his comments at the meet and greet. After that, I purposely switched focus to the trouble June and I kept having with the twins, Zach and Bradley, and keeping their names straight. That was something he could relate to.

We had arrived. There was no need for me to say another word. Hamm set his bag down and stood perfectly still, taking in the sight of the majestic sailing vessel.

"Wow, she's even more impressive up close."

Although I'd seen the ship numerous times by now, it still took my breath away. A line from John Masefields's poem, "Sea Fever," came to mind, and when I recited it out loud, Hamm smiled. After twenty-some years of marriage, he was used to my habit of using lines from literature to express my feelings when my own words seemed inadequate. "I must down to the seas again, to the lonely sea and the sky,/ And all I ask is a tall ship and a star to steer her by."

"That about sums it up," Hamm said. "Except I would ask for my loyal first mate to be at my side."

"Do you two need some alone time?" June had effectively squashed the mood. I'd have to wait to give my husband a proper welcome and thank you for his romantic gift until tonight.

"Come on then." I tugged at Hamm's collar playfully. "Wait till you see our stateroom. They pulled out all the stops. It's like staying at a luxury hotel."

We boarded the *Angel's Trumpet*, stepped onto the aft deck, and before Hamm got his bag adjusted, he was introduced to my jewel-toned, feathery nemesis. Pretty Boy swooped low, circled the deck, and headed right back toward us. He continued his aerial antics, all the while squawking in his singsong voice. On the third pass, I made out what he was saying.

"He got greedy. Broke the treaty."

"So, this is Pretty Boy. I have to admit, he's more impressive up close too. Did he say something about someone getting greedy?"

"He did." I repeated what I heard, and June confirmed she had heard the same thing. We were getting pretty fluent in parrot speak.

"I wonder if he's trying to tell us something," she continued. "Pretty Boy belonged to Chef Truffle. What treaty could he mean, and what was he getting greedy for?"

Hamm watched Pretty Boy as he made one last pass in front of us before heading out in the direction of the park. "Do you seriously think that bird was trying to help you solve a crime? FYI, his testimony wouldn't stand up in court."

June sighed. "Stranger things have happened. Animals are very intuitive, you know. It wouldn't be the first time an animal helped solve a crime."

Hamm was about to enlighten June with his own ideas on the topic of animal-assisted law enforcement when his phone rang, interrupting his train of thought. He was a traditionalist when it came to his phone. No chirping or buzzing or top-ten pop songs for him. His ringtone was the sound of an old-fashioned desk phone. I'd recognize it anywhere. I watched his expression change from concern to irritation and finally to anger as he listened to the caller. If he still had a flip-phone, he would have slammed it closed.

"What is it, Hamm? What's wrong?"

"Looks like I'll have to wait for the ship tour. I need to get back to Beacon Pointe."

Alarm bells sounded in my head. "What? Why? Did something happen to our boat? Is June's boat okay?"

"That was the marina office. Someone from our dock called in and reported there was a stranger on our boat—a young man. He got into the cabin and was down there awhile. The caller didn't notice him leaving with anything obvious, but I need to find out what's going on. I know I locked the door when I left."

"Maybe it was one of our friends," I suggested. "Greg and Lynn know where we keep the spare key."

"I hope that's all it is, but I want to make sure. Besides, the caller said it was a young man. Greg's hair hasn't been brown for a long time." I had to admit he had a point.

"There are a lot of people we don't know in the marina this weekend because of the holiday, and on top of that, most of our friends are on their own weekend trips."

My disappointment was as strong as my concern. I realized he was right. Most of the regulars on the dock made a point to leave the marina when it was overrun by guests, so it would be prime picking for someone with less than honorable intentions. "Oh, Hamm, this isn't fair. You just got here."

He sighed. "Don't I know it. I hope I get a chance to see the inside of this ship before it sets sail for good. Most likely, it'll turn out to be nothing, but I won't be able to relax unless I know what's up. If I keep taking the ferry back and forth at this rate, I could have paid for dockage."

"I'll take your bag and stow it in our room. You go check on the boat and get back here as quickly as you can. I'm going to think positive thoughts, and we'll have something to laugh about over dinner." I gave him the biggest hug I could, since I wasn't sure how long it would have to last.

He reciprocated and kissed my neck, reassuring me everything would be fine and he'd be back before I knew it. He held me at arm's length then as if to commit me to memory. "The necklace looks beautiful on you," he said.

"Don't give up the ship," I replied wistfully.

And just like that, it was back to June and me. I watched my husband's retreating figure for a long time, feeling his absence before he was out of my sight.

I had to snap out of it. First of all, I wasn't alone. I had my best friend beside me. Secondly, Hamm was just taking a thirty-minute ride across the lake, and last but not least, I looked around at the deserted deck and was struck with a brilliant idea.

"June, come on. I know what we need to do."

"So do I. Ditch the duds, retrieve our golf cart, and get over to the monument to find our next clue."

"No. Don't you see. There's no one around. Now's our perfect chance to get some answers."

"The clue leads to the monument. That's where the next answers are."

"June. Look at me." I needed to get her mind off the singular path on which it was currently fixated. "I'm not talking about the treasure hunt or following the clues. I'm saying now's our chance to check out Truffle's cabin and see if we can figure out what happened to him and why. Don't you think solving a murder is more important than winning a scavenger hunt."

That got her attention. "Why, of course it's more important. In fact, I'd like nothing more than to break the story, but I'm not so sure we should step on the toes of the law. Detective Hunk made that pretty clear. And what about Captain Stud Muffin? I don't think he'd appreciate us snooping around on his ship."

"Yes, well. Don't you think they'd both welcome the assistance? We're the ones who discovered the body. Maybe Pretty Boy showing up just now is a sign we should look into Truffle's activities a little more closely."

Once June heard my rationale, she was all in. "Maybe we can get a better idea of the relationship between Blackhart and Truffle. He says they were good friends, but that doesn't sit well with me."

I agreed. "No time like the present. Let's put Hamm's bag in the room. We can check out the dining room and hall on the way to make sure the coast is clear."

The entire ship was eerily quiet as we made our way to the stateroom. Once Hamm's duffle was safely stashed, we slipped out and padded silently down the hallway. We stopped in front of Truffle's cabin door, and I placed my hand on the door handle.

"It's unlocked," I whispered.

Chapter 11

The cabin recently occupied by the departed chef was much smaller than the guest suites. It was tidy and efficiently arranged, but I saw no personal effects such as photos, journals, or electronics. I don't know what I was expecting. The cops had already processed the scene, hence the removal of the yellow tape from the door. Any interesting personal effects were already at the police station being catalogued, examined, and checked for fingerprints. The sponsors of the contest certainly didn't want a reminder of the crime distracting the weekend guests.

I was about to open the top drawer of the dresser just in case something had been missed when I heard footsteps in the hall. The door swung inward at the same moment I dove for cover under the bed. I didn't have time to warn June. If the intruder didn't kill us—oh wait, we were the intruders—I was pretty sure I was a goner anyway. How could I leave my best friend on her own to face off with a potential murderer?

"May I ask what you're doing in here?" It was the voice of Detective Rains, and he didn't sound amused. His shoes passed in front of my face—I'd recognize those well-worn loafers anywhere. I stared at Rains's feet as I concentrated on coming up with a plan to help June escape the detective's scrutiny.

I need not have worried. Although I was the actress by trade, June could improvise on the fly with the best of them. I couldn't see her face, but her voice took on an undertone of damsel in distress.

"Oh, Detective Rains. Lucas? May I call you Lucas?" He said nothing. "Thank goodness you got here just now. I was on my way to Francie's room to see if she was ready to go, when I noticed this door was open. I peeked inside. I know I shouldn't have come in, but it just happened. And now here you are. There's no one here, and it doesn't look like anything was tampered with, so I guess I'll be on my way."

Did I just hear that? Was she going to leave me stranded under Truffle's bed while Rains tossed the room looking for evidence of a new intruder? Under the circumstances, I couldn't blame her.

"Hold on a minute. You say the door was open. Was it standing wide open, or was it merely unlocked?"

"Lucas, what are you implying?" Rains didn't object to June's use of his first name, so I guessed he was giving in to her charms.

"It's not safe for you to be nosing around in here, especially alone. You realize the killer may be on board the ship, and if he is, he's probably watching both you and Francie. Let me walk you to her room."

"Um, thanks but that won't be necessary. I'm going to visit the ladies' room first. And then I might just do a little exploring on my own. I don't want to bother Francie. Now that her husband is back, I figured they'd want some alone time. This is supposed to be their romantic anniversary weekend, you know."

I couldn't see any more of June than her ankles, but I was sure her face was all innocence and concern.

"I didn't realize that. Francie didn't mention her anniversary last night." He didn't say anything else, but from the sounds I heard, I gathered he had pulled out his notebook and was scribbling down this new information.

"Okay, but if you notice anything else out of the ordinary, call me. Don't do another thing to put yourself in harm's way or to get in the way of the investigation."

"Thanks, Lucas. I feel much better knowing you're around keeping the peace."

I smiled to myself and didn't let out a sigh of relief until I heard the door click and was certain there were no more shoes or attached bodies in the room. I wriggled out from my hiding place trying to avoid the dust bunnies, but stopped when I noticed a slip of paper. I must have been lying on it.

"What the heck?" I said aloud to the empty room. I was looking at the receipt for June's hotel room. I stuffed it in my pocket, gave the room one more cursory glance, and decided it was time to leave. I inched open the door, looked both ways, and high-tailed it to my stateroom where June was waiting for me.

"So much for my romantic rendezvous," I said.

"That was close," she said, but stopped short of congratulating ourselves on pulling a fast one over on Detective Rains. "What's the matter, Francie? You look like you've seen a ghost. Did you run into Rains? Are you mad that I said you were back here with Hamm?"

"No, no, nothing like that." I dug in my pocket and handed her the receipt.

Recognition filled her eyes. "Where did you get this? It was in my wallet. Did you find my wallet?"

Retrieving my voice, I replied, "It was under Truffle's bed—just the receipt, no wallet. And nice performance, by the way. I was worried for a minute, but you pulled it off like a pro."

"Thanks, but next time it would be nice to get a heads-up."

"Sorry. I didn't have time to do anything other than react. Do you think the killer is really on board the ship? Do you feel like we're being watched or followed? Maybe we're not being as careful about our safety as Detective Rains keeps suggesting." I looked at the receipt in June's hand. "How do you think that got under Truffle's bed?"

"One more question without an answer. We need to figure out what's going on around here."

I agreed. "You've got that right. None of this makes sense. There's got to be a connection. And as for the killer, we just need to stay on our toes. I can't imagine he's lying in wait for us. He's probably long gone. The longer he sticks around here, the more likely it is he'll be caught. If we're going to put the pieces of this puzzle together, I say we keep doing what we're doing."

We had come this far, and while my adrenalin was still in overdrive, I thought we might as well forge ahead. "While we have the chance, we might as well stop by Captain Blackhart's room. Are you in?"

June wasn't one for sitting back and waiting for things to happen. "Of course I'm in. Who wants to sit around waiting for the unknown?"

"What are we waiting for then? Let's go. And we should come up with an exit strategy in case we're caught off guard again."

"What are the odds of us getting caught snooping twice in a row?" June asked. I should have known those odds would be better than average.

I was beginning to wonder if any of the cabin doors locked properly when we located Blackhart's room and the door swung in without resistance. "Let's leave it open. That way, if we're spotted, we can say we were looking for the captain, saw his door was open, and stepped inside."

"That works," June agreed. "Usually, the simplest explanation is the best."

We crossed the threshold, careful not to touch anything, and were about to get our snoop on, when *Wham!*

Seriously? Pretty Boy's flamboyant appearances didn't even faze me anymore. But this time, his unexpected materialization was different because he wasn't squawking cryptic messages as he flew around the room. He couldn't because he was holding something in his beak. It looked to me like one of his own colorful feathers. He perched on the back of the desk chair just long enough to let out one loud caw and drop his parrot plunder on the floor before flapping out of the room. I was impressed he was able to stir up such a ruckus without breaking anything.

June stooped and picked up the gift—if that's what it was meant to be. "I was wondering where this was."

"What are you talking about? What is it?"

She held up a swatch of bright green synthetic hair attached to a clip. So, I was right about my friend's quick-change streaks, but what was Pretty Boy doing with it?

"Francie, hide!"

I didn't stop to ask. I swung open the closet door, slipped inside, and closed it seconds before Captain Blackhart strolled into the room. There were no slats in the door, so I was forced to listen and imagine the scene as it unfolded.

Blackhart sounded startled. "June, can I help you?"

"Oh, yes, Captain. There you are. I was actually looking for you when I heard a commotion coming from in here. Your door was open, and your parrot was flying around like crazy. I can't believe he didn't knock anything over."

Blackhart hesitated. "I just passed Pretty Boy sitting on the deck rail. What was he doing in here?"

"I haven't got a clue. That's what I came in to find out. He flew out leaving me standing here looking like a fool." From my hiding spot, I wondered what June had done with the clip-on hair and what the captain thought of her story.

"Well, never mind. What was it you wanted to see me about?" It sounded like he believed her.

"To be truthful, when I heard you telling Hamm all about this great ship, I got a little jealous. I was wondering if you had time to give me a tour since Hamm's not around at the moment, and I can't get in the stateroom if you know what I mean."

I cringed in the dark and could almost see her giving me the wink-wink, in reference to her last remark.

He fell for it hook, line, and, yes, sinker. I waited a few minutes to be sure they had gone before extricating myself from a tight spot for the second time in under an hour. I figured June had bought me enough time to have a quick look around, and I was certain she didn't mind spending some one-on-one time with the handsome pirate.

Where to start? I surveyed the room for general impressions. Like Truffle's cabin, the captain's room was clean and neat. Unlike the chef, Blackhart had a photo on the dresser and one on his desk. One was a group shot of the crew on the deck of the *Angel's Trumpet*. The only two people I recognized were the cabin boy and Chef Truffle complete with Pretty Boy perched on his shoulder. For an instant, I felt bad for the bird and thought of how he must miss his master.

The second photo was Captain Blackhart in civilian clothes, arms wrapped around an exotic beauty who looked familiar. I rubbed my eyes and looked again. She had amazing auburn hair that flowed over one shoulder past her waist. Her tight-fitting dress revealed much of her enviable figure in addition to part of a tattoo. It looked like a scorpion's tale, but I couldn't be sure. The rest of the artwork was covered by her clothing. They made a stunning couple. I wished I could remember where I'd seen her.

On the nightstand, I found an assortment of business cards, notes scrawled on scraps of paper, a few expired coupons, and a library card. Something wasn't adding up. On closer inspection, I noticed the notes were all written in different handwriting. The library card was familiar. It was from the Cleveland branch I frequented when I was home. I held it up for closer inspection, and a shiver ran up my spine when I saw the patron's name on the front. Juniper Sterling. Something was very wrong, and it had something to do with June's missing wallet and its contents, which were showing up in very suspicious places. There was something else niggling at the back of my mind, but since I probably wouldn't recall it until I was in bed tonight, I finished up my quick sweep of the captain's quarters. I didn't find anything suspicious in the bathroom, but I did make a mental note of the brand of Blackhart's shampoo and conditioner. Satisfied I had covered all the bases, it was time to reconnect with June and compare notes.

I found her sharing a drink with Captain Blackhart at the ship's bar. June looked content to be cozying up to the charismatic pirate about whom I was feeling very conflicted at the moment. I could have used a drink myself, but knew now was not the time or place. It was time to put on my most convincing smile and persuade my friend to leave with me.

"There you are, June. I've been looking everywhere for you. I couldn't call as you know." I turned toward Captain Blackhart and greeted him as well. "I'm sorry to interrupt, but we need to get going if we want to make it to the monument in daylight."

"The monument? I thought you were with your husband. Is this part of the treasure hunt?"

I found his question odd. He knew all the stops on the treasure hunt, and why would he care if I were with Hamm or not. Maybe since he thought Hamm was back, he could have June to himself. I chose not to remark on either.

"Thank you for the tour, Cole. I hope I can see more of the ship before the weekend's over. And thanks for the drink too." Blackhart rose from his seat as June finished off her cocktail and stood to leave. I could feel his stare on my back as we left the bar and walked down the quiet hallway toward the ship's exit.

I could hardly wait until we were out of earshot. "Cole? Really? It didn't take long for you to make it to first name status with the captain."

"I was playing a part, taking one for the team."

"Is that what you were doing with *Lucas* as well?" I was ribbing her, and she took it all in stride. "While we're on the topic of the many men in your life, have you heard anything from Michael? Or *Jack?*" Maybe that last crack was crossing a line, but I was getting a bad feeling and I couldn't shake it off.

"No, but Cole offered to send a crew member to take care of the golf cart problem. If you don't mind walking to the monument, the golf cart will be delivered to the lot reserved for guests aboard the ship, and the key will be waiting for us when we return. Not bad, huh?"

"That's good news. I'm glad we don't have to go back to the winery to pick it up. It's a much longer walk than hoofing it to the monument. Did the captain offer you any other special services while I was risking my life tossing his room?"

"How about we forget about all the gorgeous men throwing themselves at me. What did you find?"

"You're not going to like this." I handed her the library card. "This was on Blackhart's nightstand along with a lot of other random stuff—stuff you'd find in purses and wallets—receipts, lists, business cards, that kind of thing."

"How can this be? If someone found my wallet and turned it in, why didn't I get it back? And why are my things ending up all over this ship? Did you find any money or credit cards?"

"No, nothing of any real value. That's what worries me. I still don't know what's going on, but I know Blackhart is up to something."

"There are at least two separate things going on here. There's Truffle's murder, and there's missing wallets. Petty theft versus felony murder."

"Or maybe they're not separate things. Maybe they're connected. Maybe the murder was part of a theft ring. Someone got greedy. Tempers got hot."

"Pretty Boy did mention someone getting greedy."

"Oh brother. It's bad when a parrot is better at sleuthing than we are."

Chapter 12

We mulled over the strange series of today's events as we walked toward the monument, but it was impossible to remain anxious or unnerved for too long amid the festive atmosphere all around us. Caribbean and Reggae-inspired music spilled from restaurants and bars. People strolled by sporting pirate hats and eye patches, eating ice cream, and carrying bags containing souvenirs of their island vacations. Jolly Roger flags and "Don't Give Up the Ship" pennants danced in the breeze everywhere I looked.

"Do you mind if we make a quick stop here?" We were in front of one of my favorite boutiques on the island, and I couldn't resist a peek inside. Something as mundane as window-shopping might be just the ticket to give my brain a break from killers, birds, and thieves.

"No problem, but remember you can't buy anything. I'm glad you found my library card, but it's not as useful as my Visa card would have been."

"I can look though. I'm in serious need of a new purse. And I owe you a new top. If I find anything, I can have the shop hold them until Hamm comes back. This time I won't let him get away—at least not without leaving me some cash."

Inside, the boutique was cool and quiet in sharp contrast to the street. I wandered over to the purse display and was about to check out a pretty leather tote when I caught a glimpse of black hair streaked with white. There couldn't be more than one woman on this island with Marla's distinctive do. Since she was facing the opposite direction, I debated whether to walk over and say hi or pretend I didn't see her. Before I could decide, she ducked into a dressing room with an armful of clothing.

June tugged on my arm. "Psst."

"Why are you whispering?"

"Shh. Look over there." She pointed to the corner of the shop where the sale racks were located.

"I know about the sales, June. They're not secret. Did you find a top you want?"

"No, look." She was still whispering and pointing. "It's Liz, and she just grabbed that lady's wallet."

"What? Are you sure you're not being paranoid?"

"I saw it. Should we call her out on it? Maybe she's involved with whatever's going on back at the ship."

A memory flashed into my mind—Liz and Chef Truffle deep in conversation just outside the dining room on our first night. Maybe she knew something that could lead us to his killer. But what? Her only connection to the pirate ship was her mother, and she wouldn't have been with Marla if she hadn't been kicked off the swim team. She would have been with my daughter and the rest of the girls at the state campground. I tried to remember the reason for her expulsion. Did it have to do with stealing?

"Let's not make a scene," I decided. "We'll just give her the evil eye on our way out, so she can wonder whether we witnessed her crime or not."

"Yes, and whether she'll be arrested sooner rather than later. I'm thinking this might be worth reporting to Lucas."

"So it really is Lucas now, not Detective Rains?"

"Maybe," June sighed. "There's definitely something about him."

"Decisions, decisions," I said. "Let's go. I've had my fill of shopping. It's no fun without money, and I want to be gone before Marla comes out of the dressing room. I'm not in the mood for a confrontation over parenting skills."

On our way out, I shot a scathing look directly at Liz. She looked right back at me without a hint of embarrassment. On top of that, she showed no sign of recognizing me. "That was bizarre," I said.

"Which part?" June countered. "The dynamics between those Fuller ladies make my head hurt."

"True. This treasure hunt is turning out to be the easy part of the weekend."

After we left the boutique and rounded the corner, there were no more shops or pubs to distract us—nothing but green grass, a straight sidewalk, and the impressive white structure of Perry's Victory and Peace Monument up ahead. The three tall flagpoles standing sentry in front of the towering granite obelisk made this a favorite backdrop for vacation photos. A group of tourists were taking turns snapping one another's pictures as we approached. A golf cart pulled out of its parking space, made a sharp turn, and nearly ran us over.

"Hey," I yelled, "Watch where you're going!"

Bradley was in the driver's seat. He shrugged apologetically but didn't stop. Zach gave us a mock salute and shouted, "Good luck!" as they whizzed past us. He was eating popcorn, but equal numbers of kernels were being tossed into his mouth and over the side of the cart leaving a trail worthy of Hansel and Gretel.

"Looks like Zach needed an afternoon snack." I was irritated, not because he was eating, but because he evidently didn't know the problems created by leaving food where seagulls gathered.

There were white and gray gulls everywhere I looked, and more were arriving every second. Zach and Bradley must have been enjoying their snack right under the flagpoles because we couldn't get near them. The popcorn was creating a force field that could not be penetrated until the gulls had gobbled up every last kernel and taken off in search of their next food fest.

June gave the receding golf cart a look of disdain. "I'm guessing the guys found something under the flag poles, but there's no way we can check out the spot until these scavengers finish their meal. I wonder if they scattered the popcorn there on purpose to slow the rest of us down, or if they're just oblivious. Either way, it worked."

"We might as well start at the back of the monument," I suggested. "Maybe we'll scare the gulls off when we start walking around." Even as I said it, I knew it would never happen. Seagulls were as tenacious as they were attractive.

June followed me as I headed toward the concrete stairs surrounding the tall, white column. I turned around in time to see her stop short, lean forward, and put her hands on her knees. For a second, I thought she might throw up. I needn't have worried, though. She clapped her hands and shouted, "Here boy! Here Gunner!"

The German shepherd bounded joyfully toward my friend, leash flapping behind him. His master followed at a slower pace now that he'd released his hold on his faithful companion. I marveled once again at June's ability to attract males of all species.

By the time Michael caught up to Gunner, the dog was sitting at attention. "Hi there, ladies. Out for a late afternoon stroll or stirring up more trouble?" He indicated the flock of seagulls tripping over each other, vying for tidbits of abandoned food."

"We are not to blame for this one," I announced. "We're finishing up our treasure hunt for today. Our last clue led us here, but we can't get near the flagpoles because of them." I nodded toward the birds who didn't look like they were leaving anytime soon.

"Maybe I can help." Michael walked up to Gunner and commanded, "*Verfolgungsjagd*!"

Gunner immediately jumped up and ran right into the middle of the munching mob, barking and chasing after the gulls until every one of them was gone.

"Wow. Thanks." I was impressed. "Your dog speaks German?"

"He doesn't speak it, but he does understand commands," Michael replied. "He is German, you know." A rare smile softened the chiseled features of the man who seemed to turn up in the right places at the right times.

With the birds out of the way, we were free to explore the area. June stopped beneath the three towering flagpoles—one each for the USA, Canada, and Britain. The monument and the flagpoles were there to remind visitors to celebrate the long-lasting peace among Britain, Canada, and the U.S. and to honor those who fought in the Battle of Lake Erie during the War of 1812.

She circled each pole looking carefully at the ground. I joined her, stopping to pick up discarded popcorn kernels in the hopes of avoiding a repeat performance by the scavenger birds. When I reached the landscaped area at the base of the flagpoles, I noticed something shiny glinting among the white stones. I kicked around in the rocks with the toe of my sneaker.

I reached down and retrieved the object. It was a small pouch made of a flimsy silver fabric. Inside the pouch were four shiny quarters. I didn't have my reading glasses on me, so I handed the coins over to June for further inspection.

"These are pretty cool," she said, fingering the silver coins. "They're all different though. Only one's an actual U.S. quarter. It's a 2013 from the America the Beautiful quarter series. It's the Ohio coin with Commodore Perry on the back standing in front of this monument."

"Since when did you become such an expert on coins?"

She handed the quarter to me pretending she didn't know I couldn't make out the figure, let alone the fine print. That's what friends do. "I'm no numismatist, but Sterling had a thing for silver. I picked up on it by association."

She was referring to her ex-husband, Clifton Sterling. I considered him a pompous buffoon for the most part, but he was handsome, intelligent, and the face of the six o'clock news on the third-ranked TV station in Cleveland. Unfortunately, it wasn't until after they had tied the knot, June discovered he was more like an irresponsible, self-centered child than a professional newsman. I watched as she inspected the second coin, which was similar in size to the first. It was Canadian. I could tell the difference between a man and a moose, even without my glasses. It stood to reason the next one would be British. Again, the size and color was close to the familiar American quarter dollar. Queen Elizabeth looked more like President Washington than the moose, but the crown on her head gave it away. I was getting good at this guessing game. It was a standard, ten-pence British coin.

"Okay, those three make sense—one each for the three countries represented by the flags here—but what's the fourth coin?" I asked. June was holding it up to the fading light and squinting intently.

"I think it's the next clue. Give me another second. There are words on both sides."

I moved in closer, as if standing shoulder-to-shoulder would help her read the tiny words with greater ease.

"Vessel without hinges, key or lid," is what it says on this side.

"Flip it over," I encouraged. "What does it say on the back?"

"Settle down, Francie. I've got this."

I backed off, realizing I was trying to compensate for my farsightedness by talking louder.

After more squinting and scrunching of eyebrows and lips, June divulged the second half of the clue. "Yet golden treasure inside is hid."

" Read the whole thing together, would you?"

"Vessel without hinges, key or lid, yet golden treasure inside is hid."

"So, it's not referring to the treasure; it's the container or vessel holding it," I mused.

"I agree. So what kind of lidless container holds golden treasure? Treasure chests typically have lids and hinges."

"Yes," I added, "They have locks needing keys, too. While we're thinking, we should poke around here a bit more. Maybe there's something else hidden in these rocks that'll help us put it all together." I sank to my knees and rooted around in the landscaping stone. With my back to June, I wiped perspiration from my forehead and lifted the hair off my neck to catch a passing breeze.

"Look, Francie, here's a stone that's not a real stone." She held up an egg-shaped object bigger than the other stones. "It's one of those plastic Easter eggs people put candy in for egg hunts."

"Open it. Open it! What's inside?"

She popped the white, plastic egg at the seam, lifted out a strip of paper with printed instructions on it, and read it aloud.

"Which came first, the chicken or the egg? It doesn't really matter, just shake a leg. Do the chicken dance at the Chicken Patio. Record it, and share it, and there you go. You will earn five bonus coins toward the treasure hunt for this activity."

"Eggs. Chickens. Chickens. Eggs. There's something to this." The answer to this riddle was just beyond reach.

June was already practicing her dance moves. "This could be fun. Nothing like a dance party to get the creative juices flowing." She was flapping her elbows and hopping in place.

"Wait!" I commanded. "Back up. I figured out the riddle. The answer is 'egg.' It all makes sense."

June stopped her dance and gave me a look. "Egg? That's what you've got? And how does it all make sense?"

"Think about it. The vessel is an eggshell. No lid, no hinges, no key. The golden treasure is the yolk inside."

"Okay. So it makes sense, but so what? Where does that lead us, except maybe back to your berth on the sailboat, Mrs. *Egg*."

"Seriously, June? You're going there?"

"I'm sorry. I just don't see how an egg can be a clue on this treasure hunt. It's making me crazy."

"Maybe it's as simple as the plastic egg you're holding. Kind of like the clues at the winery. They go together. The second ones are probably to make sure people eventually get where they need to be."

"Okay, I'll bite. So, you're saying our next destination is the Chicken Patio?"

"Why not?" I decided I wasn't going to allow myself to feel defeated over a silly riddle. I decided we should be celebrating. I stood up straight, brushed off my clothes and fluffed my damp hair.

"I think we've solved the riddle. We found the egg. The clue in it leads to the Chicken Patio. Doing the chicken dance when we get there is just for bonus points."

"I guess I could eat," June said. "All this walking and sleuthing and flirting has made me hungry."

"I second that. Chicken Patio here we come."

Chapter 13

I f we weren't hungry when we left the monument, by the time we walked back to the center of town and arrived at the Chicken Patio, that had all changed. The smell of the outdoor grills and the secret barbecue sauce had my mouth watering. We headed straight to the food line to place our orders.

"Hi! I see you're wearing an *Angel's Trumpet* treasure hunt wristband. That's great. Here are your instructions." The enthusiastic grill minder handed me a printed sheet and turned back to his chicken.

"Thanks. I'd like to place an order for..."

"I'm sorry ma'am. You need to follow the instructions on the handout." He smiled brightly and added, "Have a great day, and good luck on the treasure hunt!"

"What the? Are you hearing this, June?"

"I am. It sucks, but he may have just saved you a big embarrassment."

"What's that supposed to mean?"

"It means—you have no money. How were you planning to pay for dinner?"

"Dang. You've got me there. Let's look at the handout and see what we have to do. Maybe they'll reward us with a snack when we're done."

The instructions were clear. Each team was to gather at least six people and convince them to join in a flash mob performance of the Chicken Dance. Music would be provided by the person in the yellow suit standing next to the barbecue station. June and I looked over to the grills, and sure enough, there was a young woman wearing a bright yellow dress with yellow and red striped tights. On a nearby table were a small sound system, speakers, and a portable microphone, along with some chicken-themed props. I didn't notice her earlier because she wasn't the only person in the area wearing an outlandish outfit. Anything goes on holiday weekends and celebrations at Put-in-Bay.

Turning our focus back to the instructions, we learned we'd need a volunteer to record the dance. After the performance, all guest participants were required to sign the form on the back of the handout agreeing to the release of the video for promotional purposes. Finally, we were to share our presentation on the Paradise Rum Pirates Facebook page and tweet it using #paradisepirates and #chickendance. The team with the most likes, shares, and retweets would win additional points toward determining the treasure hunt winner. Upon uploading the video to Facebook, a link would be provided to the final clue, and a gift certificate for dinner at one of the sponsor restaurants would be awarded.

It was the last line that got me excited. Dinner was in our future, and we wouldn't have to beg or steal. All we needed to do was sing for our supper.

"We've got this in the bag, June. I don't really see Zach and Bradley going all out on this one. And I can just imagine Marla trying to convince Liz to suit up and shake her tail feathers with mother hen."

June laughed out loud at the mental picture. "We're going to blow them away. They won't stand a chance. I'll gather our back-up dancers while you go pick out our outfits and get our music cued up.

Thanks to June's powers of persuasion, the party atmosphere, and the abundance of pirate weekend revelers, not to mention the free-flowing alcohol, we had a dance team assembled in no time. I passed out feathers, beaks, and a few chicken feet, provided some simple instructions, and got everyone to sign the release form. We were ready to rock. I took one last look at our motley cast and hesitated. I hoped Pretty Boy didn't fly by and think I had concocted an elaborate courting ritual. The bird seemed to have me on radar, turning up wherever I went. There was no turning back now. I gave the thumbs up sign, and we rocked the best rendition of the Chicken Dance in recent history.

The crowd erupted in applause when we took our final bow. Shouts of *Encore*! and *Bravo*! punctured the warm summer air. June and I obliged our new fans with a few extra tail shakes and elbow flaps for good measure. The deed was done.

Two members of our makeshift dance party hung back after the others drifted off to their next holiday adventure. "Bill and I would like to buy you some nachos and margaritas. We haven't had this much fun in years. Thanks for reminding us how to embrace the moment."

"The pleasure is ours," I said. "It was fun, wasn't it?"

So, once again, food and refreshments appeared just in the nick of time. We exchanged island stories with our new friends Bill and Tonia. We laughed about tonight's entertainment, approved the video, and sipped our drinks while June expertly completed the tasks of uploading, sharing, and tweeting.

We finished our refreshments and thanked Bill and Tonia again for being part of our dance team and for sharing some snacks and time with us. They walked across the street into the park arm in arm.

"They're a great couple, aren't they?"

"You and Hamm are every bit as great, you know. I hope someday I find the guy I want to walk with into the sunset."

"And give up the single life?" I asked.

Ping! Our conversation ended, saving June from having to respond. There was an incoming message on her phone.

She opened it and shared its contents with me. "There's a message and an attachment. The message is the last clue. The attachment is a certificate for dinner for two at The Goat Soup and Whiskey Tavern."

"Hamm and I love The Goat! It's our favorite restaurant on the island." I felt a twinge of loneliness and a second one of worry. "I hope he calls soon to let me know what's going on at the marina. I don't like the idea of a stranger on the boat. In spite of all the security, it's scary that someone can just show up like that."

"The security is good at Beacon Pointe. That's why I think it had to be someone you know. Let's take a look at this clue. It'll get your mind off the other stuff, and I'm sure Hamm will call or text my phone with good news for you as soon as he can."

"Okay. Let's have it." Worrying wasn't going to change or accomplish anything, so I might as well focus on something I could act on.

"I don't like this one." June stared at her phone screen as if willing the message to change. "It sounds sinister to me."

I pressed her to read the clue, so she did. "Weight in my belly. Trees on my back. Nails in my ribs. Feet I do lack."

I agreed. It did sound darker than the others, but I thought I knew the answer right away.

"The answer to the riddle is a ship. That's the easy part. The hard part is it's impossible to know which ship. There are hundreds of ships docked here this weekend, and boats are pulling in and out all day and night."

"I'm really impressed with your puzzle-solving skills, Francie. You've figured out every one of the clues. Maybe you should become an investigator after all."

"I've thought about going back to school now that the kids are out of the nest. I love my career, but there's always been a tiny part of me that wonders what more I could become."

"The sky's the limit."

I laughed recalling the sight of my friend dropping out of the sky onto my lawn. But that's a story for another day.

"We'll have to think about this one," June said, getting back to the problem at hand. "Maybe there's a ship of some kind that never leaves the island."

"While we're on the topic of ships, we should go back and wash up and change for dinner. I refuse to show up late and miss out on the best meal of the weekend, free or otherwise."

"Don't you want to wait awhile and see if Hamm gets back so you can go with him instead of me?"

"Are you kidding? We're going to get ready and go to dinner. Keep your phone on you, and if he calls I'll tell him to meet us there. He'll have money for his food. You've been at this all day with me, and you deserve a nice meal."

"Okay, you don't have to twist my arm. I'm ready for a change of clothes and a sit-down dinner. Since this is a sponsored event, I'm sure we'll be sitting with the other four. I'd like to find out more about what was going on in the boutique earlier before deciding whether or not to turn Liz in."

We made our way back to the ship, using the time to discuss each of the people we'd met since our arrival. There were plenty of details to go over, and by talking about them maybe we would recall some piece of information that would prove critical to the investigation—not that we were actually involved in the investigation. It seemed like no time at all before we were striding down the hall toward our cabin. We were still deep in conversation, when we stopped to unlock the door.

"...Yes, and I'd like to remind Zach and Bradley about respecting the environment, and by that I mean not causing a seagull apocalypse with popcorn."

"What would you like to talk to me about exactly?"

I jumped at the sound of the voice behind me. Where in the heck had he come from?

"You scared me half to death, Zach."

The hallway leading to the guest rooms was shadowy, and Zach was wearing dark glasses, so I couldn't be sure, but if I had to guess, I'd be willing to bet he was rolling his eyes. The thing I was sure about was he was emanating bad vibes in all directions. Why was he leaning against the wall casually cutting slices from an apple with a knife that looked too sharp for the job at hand?

"Well?" he asked "what lesson were you going to teach me, Professor?"

"I was just going to mention that seagulls are a big menace around here, and we try to keep them from gathering in large numbers and causing destruction by not feeding them. That's all. I didn't mean to sound like I was going to lecture you or something. Sorry if it sounded that way."

"Hmm. I'll keep that in mind. See you at dinner."

I couldn't shut the door soon enough. "Call me paranoid if you want, but I'm exhausted from worrying about being stabbed in the back at every turn."

"A little paranoia can be a good thing sometimes. Let's get ready and give Pervis a call to drive us to dinner. I bet we can put the cab fare on your tab. After everything we've been through, Captain Blackhart wouldn't dare begrudge you a few bucks for transportation. We won't have to think about golf carts or keys, or driving back in the dark."

I agreed with June's suggestion. Tonight we could relax, have a few drinks with dinner, and not worry about who would drive back. We might even make some headway in our amateur investigation.

Pervis picked us up in his bright green taxi van and helped us into the backseat. Before we set out, I explained about the payment situation, and Pervis didn't hesitate to assure us his services would be taken care of. I was tempted to hug the kind gentleman. The ride wouldn't take long, but June and I could use the time to inquire about Zach's strange behavior at the meet and greet and our encounter on the ship. Maybe Pervis could offer some information that would help June with her news story, or maybe even help solve a murder. In the end, all we got out of him was that on Zach's recent visits, Pervis always dropped him off at a small house on the back side of the island precisely at five thirty p.m. and picked him up three hours later. Part of his popularity was evidently his reputation for being not only a gentleman, but also someone who could be trusted to be discreet.

The short ride ended at the front entrance to the Goat Soup and Whiskey Tavern. We thanked Pervis for his service, and promised we'd call him again if we needed anything. He tipped his top hat, wished us a pleasant evening, and drove away.

While we waited in the restaurant foyer for the hostess to verify our certificate and locate our server, June walked up to the series of old photographs lining the wall and became engrossed. She stuck her face so close to one I thought she might leave a nose print.

I had to pull her away when my name was called. "What was so fascinating? You looked like you were in a trance staring at those old photographs."

"I didn't realize they were pictures of the fire at the Hotel Victory. I don't come here often, but I never paid attention to them before."

"I feel dumb now. I never heard of the Hotel Victory until you showed me that article you found. Hamm and I come here at least once per visit to the island, sometimes more. I guess I'm always focused on the food and trying to decide what to order. I never paid much attention to the lobby decor. Besides, most people are drawn to the giant stuffed goat in the dining room and walk right past the photographs to check out the mascot."

We were led to a reserved table in the main dining room. In spite of the rustic, casual atmosphere, complete with stuffed creatures on all four walls, there were white tablecloths, linen napkins, and fresh flowers on the tables. With three gardens on the premises, the bouquets always reflected the beauty of the season.

One of the chefs hurried past us holding a pair of kitchen shears. He was on his way out to the herb garden just beyond the patio. Fresh vegetables were also grown on site, so whatever entree you chose, you could be assured only the finest locally sourced ingredients would be used in preparing your meal. In addition, the bread was baked in the kitchen, and the desserts were all prepared from scratch. Even the bar used only the freshest fruit, vegetables, and herbs in their wonderful original cocktails. Hamm's favorite was the basil mojito. I'm a big fan of their Cosmo.

We were the first to be seated at the round table set for eight. Since there were only six of us competing in the treasure hunt, I wondered aloud who the other settings were for.

"I'm guessing Captain Blackhart will be joining us, or at least stopping by for a drink. He's been checking in all day during or after each new step of the treasure hunt." June ran her fingers through her hair. Her pink streak was still in place and matched the pink flowers of her print halter dress. She would look right at home in the patio garden.

"Maybe the last seat is for Hamm in case he shows up," I added hopefully. I had pulled my curls into a high ponytail, letting random locks fall where they may. Hamm always says he likes it that way, and it was an easy way to catch a breeze on the back of my neck. I too had chosen a dress for tonight—solid navy, sleeveless, with a low-cut back. Classic and comfortable in case I opted for dessert.

We were perusing the menu and sipping our drinks—a Cosmo for me and a margarita for June—when Zach and Bradley were shown to their seats. Before we finished our hellos, Marla and Liz joined us. Conversation started out relaxed and impersonal, and since we were brought together by our fondness for cooking and love of the islands, it was easy to focus on the various entrees, house specialties, and unique soup menu without dwelling on our competition or our suspicions—at least for now. I was glad to see everyone seemed to be acting normally again.

The six of us ordered our meals, and I thought we might get through an entire group gathering without disruption or drama. But then I thought about the unanswered questions June and I had for our shipmates. This meal might be the last chance to find out about these people and what, if anything, they could bring to the backstory of Chef Truffle and the issue of disappearing wallets. I made up my mind. It was now or never.

"So, Marla, what did you end up buying at the boutique this afternoon?" I asked innocently enough.

She nearly choked on her meatball. While she dabbed red sauce from the corners of her mouth, I added, "I saw you going into the dressing room with an armload of stuff. It looked like you were on a mission, so I didn't want to bother you. I know I can never leave that shop without making several purchases.

Unfortunately, all I could do today was browse since I didn't have any money."

Marla recovered, and while we chatted about shorts and swimsuits, I kept stealing glances at her daughter. I saw June was keeping a steady eye on Liz as well, and the younger Fuller was growing increasingly fidgety.

"So, Liz, You were there too, right?" June was going in for the kill. "I wasn't sure it was you at first because you were with another lady. I got confused when I saw you with her wallet."

I thought Marla was going to suffer from whiplash the way her head spun. Liz's eyes were bigger than the plate in front of her. Both of them were speechless. I couldn't wait to hear what would come next.

Captain Blackhart swept through the room and landed in one of the empty seats at our table with a theatrical flourish. I was impressed by his entrance but disappointed by his timing. Nothing in his demeanor indicated he noticed the distress on either Marla's or Liz's face. I guess we'd have to figure out a different way to get some answers from Liz.

"Good evening all. It's so nice to see everyone gathered together again this evening. I hope you were all pleasantly surprised by our dinner arrangements. June, I see you chose the house margarita. It's my absolute favorite. I hope you ordered the blackened mahi mahi. They pair together magnificently. I dined here just the other night with my crew." The corners of his mouth took a downward turn. Perhaps he was remembering sharing one of the last meals with his "friend" Truffle. I don't know how every ice cube in June's margarita didn't melt on the spot after the smoldering look Cole Blackhart gave her.

Without looking the least bit scorched, June answered, "I actually went with the perch tacos. They're made every day from fresh-caught yellow perch; the breading is very light—just the way I like it; and they're fried to perfection. They're killer! Um, I mean they're really good."

Did she do that on purpose? We needed to get our game plan together because I couldn't be sure if my naturally curious friend was trying to get a reaction from the captain by implying murder or just trading flirty banter with the man. My train of thought was interrupted by the raspberry mojito that appeared in front of me no sooner than I set my empty Cosmo glass on the table.

"Compliments of the captain," the waiter said as he placed the pretty pink glass in front of me and a second margarita in front of June.

I took a sip from the frosty glass while conversations buzzed around me. Blackhart was monopolizing the conversation with my friend so I sat back to observe all my shipmates. My complimentary mojito was delicious, but the more I drank of the cocktail, the more I felt I needed to cool down. The air in the restaurant felt supercharged. I needed to check with our waiter about dimming the lights. I never needed sunglasses indoors before, but my hand shot to my side to retrieve them from my purse. Ugh! Once again, I had to come to grips with its untimely demise. I vowed to myself, since no one was paying me much attention, that one way or another I would replace my bag tonight. I fanned my face with my napkin, eyed my empty glass, and helped myself to June's second margarita. She only had eyes for Blackhart, so I didn't need to explain my sudden thirst. I couldn't cool down, even after draining the shanghaied drink and chomping the ice cubes. I needed some air.

Chapter 14

The evening air kissed my face. I had only planned to step outside for a moment, but the cool air from the lake was calling to me. I made my way to the end of the road where the land met the beckoning lake. It occurred to me I should have waited for my steak to arrive before taking a solo stroll to the water's edge. I would be quick. I only needed to cool off and clear my head. There was so much on my mind, but I couldn't seem to focus on a single thought long enough to get anywhere.

I looked down into the shallow water. Minnows were darting back and forth—maybe trying to get somewhere important or perhaps trying to avoid becoming dinner for a larger fish. A song popped into my head. *I've got my mind set on you.* George Harrison's lyrics were playing on repeat in my subconscious.

A catfish with long curly whiskers and a menacing grin joined the underwater party. *I've got my mind set on you, but it's gonna take money. A whole lot of spending money...* Was that scaly aquatic gentleman taunting me? He seemed to be mouthing the lyrics in time to my humming. Did he know something about my purse? Was there some underwater fish mafia stealing purses and ridiculing the unfortunate souls who could no longer access their most important belongings? I would not stand for this. I wanted these mutinous fish to answer for their wrongdoings. I leaned as far over the water as gravity allowed until I felt myself falling. I was floating in the realm between wakefulness and dreaming—that place where reality and fantasy change places at will. I was still holding my breath when I woke up tearing my way through layer after layer of downy comforters and silky sheets.

I was alone in my room on the ship. The sun hadn't set completely. A sliver of rose light snuck under the lowered shade that didn't quite meet the bottom of the screened porthole. I ran my hands over the cool sheets beneath me then over my midsection and up to my head. I was in one piece and all my body parts were intact. I was finally cool, thanks to the light September breeze coming in through the open screen. The only thing I was having trouble with was the origin of the gritty substance all around me on the bed. Was it dirt from the shore? I slid cautiously to the edge of the bed and sat up, aware of new aches and pains I couldn't account for. I remembered sitting down to dinner at The Goat and stepping outside for some air, but try as I might, the rest of the evening was like looking through a smudged window into my memories. I tried to pick out even one distinct event from earlier, but nothing came into focus. As I scoured my memory for something tangible, I pinched a crumb between my index finger and thumb and brought it close to my face. What was this stuff? Surely it would trigger something to help me fill in the blanks. It smelled sweet, yet there was something off-putting about the scent. When I recognized it, I was more confused than before. It was rum cake—Triple X rum cake to be specific. How did this happen? If I had managed to get my hands on a piece of Marla's prize-winning dessert, I would at least appreciate the memory of eating it. On the bright side, I was in one piece and able to move of my own accord. However I got the cake, it didn't seem I had to fight anyone for it. I stepped out of bed and brushed off the crumbs deciding a hot shower would do me more good than lying in a bed littered with cake remnants.

When the supply of hot water had run its course, I reluctantly stepped from the comforting fog into the suite I should have been sharing with my husband. It was just as I had left it, cake crumbs and all. The scene made me uneasy, so I dressed quickly with comfort in mind. Black yoga pants, tank top and a light sweatshirt would be the extent of my fashion exertion for the moment. I was debating whether or not to plug in the hair dryer when June burst through the cabin door with Detective Rains in tow.

"Thank goodness, Francie, you're here! I've been looking everywhere for you. Where did you go? I thought you were just stepping out for some air, but when the entrees came and you didn't come back, I panicked. Are you ill?"

She had to stop throwing questions at me to catch her breath, and when she did, she was taken aback by the appearance of the disheveled bed sheets. "What's going on here? And what's that stuff all over the bed?"

I was standing in the bathroom doorway with a towel in one hand and hair dryer in the other. "I'm still trying to figure it all out myself. I can't remember what happened after I left the restaurant. So far, the only thing I've figured out is that my bed is covered in cake crumbs, and seeing that I'm starving, I'm not even sure whether or not I ate the cake. Come to think of it, I can't believe I skipped dinner. Whatever made me leave, it must have been important. You know how I feel about skipping meals."

"Yes I do. That's what worried me most. And for the record, I missed dinner too. I set off to look for you before I ate mine."

Rains was silent, but the twinkle in his eye as he divided his attention between June and me led me to believe he was more amused than angry or suspicious.

"No offense, but what's he doing here?" I nodded toward the detective noticing for the first time he was holding a familiar-looking shoe casually at his side.

June let out a sigh. "I ran into him halfway between the restaurant and the shore."

Rains took the cue and picked up the story from there. He explained how he ran into June and offered to help with her search. As he spoke he extended his hand toward me. I accepted the shoe without comment, and didn't move to place it with its mate until he finished speaking. I learned June had found my shoe not far from the restaurant, which explained why my ankle hurt, and my back was sore, but how did I not remember I'd been hopping around on one foot? In addition, the manager at a nearby establishment reported a strange woman with one shoe who stole a winning rum cake he had on display and ran off yelling that the fish owed it to her. Rains and June pieced together a few more details and eventually found their way back to the *Angel's Trumpet* and my cabin. By the time they finished their story, I was equal parts mortified and terrified.

June picked up on my mood and gently guided me to the side chair where I slumped. My head felt like an iron anchor as it came to rest on my tired knees. As much as I appreciated the kindness of my friend and the efficiency of the detective, I missed my husband. I sensed that none of this would have happened if he had been here. Our romantic anniversary weekend was turning into a nightmare of epic proportion.

I didn't get the chance to drown in my swill of embarrassment, fear, and anger because when I took my hands away from my eyes to massage my throbbing temples, I noticed a plastic grocery bag sticking out from under the bed. "What's this? I don't recognize this bag. I didn't have it when I went out earlier."

I retrieved the sack, stood, and dumped its contents onto the bed. Four empty wallets, an eye patch, a bird feather, a pair of knock-off designer sunglasses, and a local newspaper created a colorful collage but triggered no further memories except that I had been determined to replace my handbag. It was a crumb (no pun intended), but it was a start. After examining each of the items for clues or identifying properties and finding nothing of value, we conceded that time and rest were the only things left I could do in hopes of shedding some light on this latest mystery.

Once Rains was satisfied I wasn't planning to leave my room and June promised to stay with me for the night, he took his leave. "Don't worry ladies, we'll get to the bottom of this soon. Getting a good night's sleep is the best thing you can do for now. I'll check in tomorrow morning, but if you remember anything or experience any other unusual events, promise you'll call me right away."

June plopped on the bed and mooned at the space vacated by Detective Rains. I appreciated her feelings, but I had more pressing things on my mind. "First things first. I don't know about you, but I'm starving. I'm calling down to the galley and ordering dinner. They can put it on my tab."

"Huh? Oh, great idea. Especially since you don't have a tab. All expenses paid, remember?"

"Oh, yeah. Brilliant. I'll get enough for both of us. Snacks too. What would you like? I'll eat anything except rum cake. There will be no more rum cake—award-winning or not, I don't care to see another piece of rum cake as long as I live."

"You know me, I'll eat anything."

I gave her a thumbs-up. June pulled out her iPad and before long, I could tell she was deep into her research. Aside from the story she was working on, I hoped she might come across some information that could help us get a handle on our current situation. Still feeling the effects from my weird memory lapse, I felt it best not to interrupt her. Instead, I borrowed June's cell phone and dialed Hamm's number, but when he didn't pick up, I had to settle on leaving him a voicemail. I tried to sound cheery and let him know I missed him and couldn't wait to see him, but after clicking off, I worried I sounded more like a desperate crazy lady trying to hang on to sanity than a devoted wife.

After nearly an hour of eating my fill and lounging on the bed next to my friend, I felt the need to do something productive, and decided to give the grocery bag and its contents another look. The wallets didn't offer up any clues other than two of them belonged to women and the other two were men's billfolds. The eye patch could have come from a hundred different places. I had a feeling I recognized the bird feather. The sunglasses didn't look familiar, but they were cute and would probably come in handy. The last thing in the plastic sack was the local newspaper. I unfolded it on my lap and scanned the stories. For the first time in a long while, I laughed out loud. June looked up from her notes.

"What is it? Are you okay? Did you remember something funny? Funny is good. Funny is better than scary or creepy."

"No, I didn't remember anything else. I was just going through this shopping bag. A few things look vaguely familiar, but I don't remember anything specific. It's these stories. I couldn't write this badly if I was trying. And the topics are just as bad. Listen to this headline. This is the lead-in on the front page." I held up the paper so June would see I wasn't making this up. "Stinky Plant Causes Library Evacuation."

"Well, it's got my attention. What's it about? Is it for real, or is it an attention grabber?"

"I haven't read the article yet. I have to stop laughing first."

June and Rains were right. Rest and a good laugh with my best friend were already working their magic. Maybe a good night's sleep would be the final ingredient in the recipe to restore the gap in my memory.

Before turning in for the night, I stacked our dinner dishes and opened the door to set them in the hall for the room service attendant. Zach was standing directly in front of our doorway looking almost as shocked to see me as I was to see him. The dishes clattered to the carpet in an untidy heap, but at least nothing broke.

"What are you doing here?" I squeaked. "Were you about to knock on our door?"

He stared at me as if trying to decide whether or not to answer me. "Uh, no. I was just waiting for my brother. We were going to go into town for a drink before turning in for the night. There's a lot going on downtown, and this is the first time all day we didn't have to be somewhere or do something connected to the contest. He forgot his credit card and had to go back to the room. If it bothers you that I'm waiting here, I can move."

"Oh. Sorry about that. Okay then. You guys have fun and be careful. You never know what kind of danger is lurking around here anymore." I wasn't sure if he caught the sarcasm in my warning, as he was the one currently lurking, but Bradley was back with his credit card in hand. Zach gave me a nod and headed down the hall with his twin.

June looked up from her project. "You were out in the hall for a long time. What took you so long?"

"I just caught Zach skulking outside our door. Am I imagining it, or do you think he was spying on us?"

"You're not imagining it. He hasn't been right since running into Pervis at the meet and greet. Those brothers are starting to give me the creeps. It's not just the fact I can't keep their names straight, either."

"Yep," I agreed. "I don't know what they think we know that they don't. In fact, it seems like they're always one step ahead of us—at least when it comes to the treasure hunt."

"We were the ones who stumbled on Chef Truffle's body," June reminded me as if I could forget. "If the brothers are involved, maybe they think we found something on the scene. It's exhausting thinking everyone is watching us all the time and not being able to trust anyone."

I wondered out loud about the new information Pervis had revealed to us in his cab. "Zach is hiding something and it has to do with his secret trips to the island leading up to this weekend. If it was purely academic research, don't you think he would have been happy to impress us with his findings?"

"You're right. Most brainy types don't pass up an opportunity to showcase their knowledge. No offense."

"Huh? What are you implying?"

"Oh, nothing, Miss Island Trivia Know-it-All."

If I couldn't tell June was kidding, I would have smacked her.

"I'm certain Pervis knows a lot more than he felt compelled to share this evening. I think we should take him up on his offer to be at our service. I'm feeling much better now, and I've gotten a second wind. I'm calling us a cab."

Chapter 15

We were waiting for the green van when it pulled to a stop at the curb. I had instructed Pervis to pick us up at the ferry dock—close enough to where the *Angel's Trumpet* was moored, but far enough to keep out of sight of prying eyes. We decided it would be best if no one from the ship saw us meeting up with Pervis, plus we promised Detective Rains we would stay in our room for the night. There was no need to go borrowing trouble.

"Where to, my ladies?" I could see the twinkle in the old gentleman's eyes reflected in his rearview mirror.

"We'd like you to take us to the house where Zach has been spending so much time on his recent island junkets."

Pervis turned in his seat to face us. "And here I thought you'd be wanting to go clubbing, or at least maybe looking for an out-of-the-way beach to do a little nature swimming."

I was surprised he didn't pull a muscle with the exaggerated wink he offered us. In spite of his surprise, or perhaps disappointment, he expressed no objections to my request, put the van in gear, and drove off.

He said it would be a quick ride to the lakeside cottage located away from the bustle of downtown on a sparsely populated lane. I was happy to hear it was not far because we were running up a tab, and I still hadn't mentioned to Captain Blackhart that he would be paying our travel expenses. Pervis didn't mention payment for this trip or our previous one, but I didn't want to take advantage.

On the way, I asked Pervis if he knew who owned the house or if anyone lived in it. Being an island native, he would have the ins and outs on most all the property owners and residents. I was hoping he'd be willing to share. I guessed he could tell us a thing or two about Lucas Rains and his recent transfer from Chicago to the islands too, but we needed to concentrate on one thing at a time. We didn't want to give him the impression we were nosy busybodies.

"The house is owned by the South Bass Island Historical Society, but Ms. Conner has lived in it since she was a little girl. When her mother passed away, she stayed on and took over her job as the village historian. No one on the island remembers anyone but the Conner ladies ever living there. Miss Bea doesn't get many visitors anymore, so I was glad when Zach started coming around last April. She's a friendly soul and has a lot of interesting stories to share with anyone who cares about the past. She lives alone and doesn't leave her house much."

"Do you think she knows anything about the fire at the Hotel Victory?" I asked about the first historical topic that entered my head.

"Of course! That and everything else that's happened on this island for the past two hundred years. You can ask her all about it yourself. Here we are. You gals have a nice visit with Bea. Call me if you need a ride back to town when you're ready."

"Thanks so much, Pervis." I had already decided not to take further advantage of his generosity. He could be transporting paying customers instead of hauling our broke behinds around town. It would be an easy walk back to the marina from here, and it would be nice to use the time taking in the lights and sights and talking about whatever we might discover from the owner of this quaint historical home. June and I waved goodbye casually and waited for him to pull away. As soon as the green van was out of sight, we walked to the front porch and knocked on the door, deciding for once, to take the direct approach.

After about a minute, June knocked again, harder this time. When there was still no answer, I began to wonder if we should have asked Pervis to wait until we were inside before he left.

June cracked her knuckles and bounced on the balls of her feet. "Looks like no one's home. Just our luck this would be the one time Ms. Conner gets invited to a party, or a poetry reading, or whatever it is spinsters do in their spare time. What should we do? Should we go around back and see if there's a window we can look in?"

"Settle down. Let's give her another minute. I'm not feeling well enough to go crawling through bushes and snooping around."

Maybe this whole trip was a bad idea after all. June may have been impatient, but as much as I hated to admit it, I was starting to feel defeated and was just about to suggest heading back when the porch light snapped on, bathing us in a weak halo of yellow light. We both snapped to attention.

"Yes, can I help you?" It became immediately clear why it took so long for Ms. Conner to come to the door. If the woman was a day under ninety, I would be surprised. She stood at her front door with only a wobbly walker to steady her wobbly frame. In contrast to her frail-looking body, there was nothing feeble about her face. The arches of her pencil-thin painted-on eyebrows were stretched nearly to her snowy white hairline, and her puckered lips told me we had better have a good reason for beckoning her to the door.

I realized too late we should have thought this through, so rather than standing here feeling naked under Ms. Conner's scrutiny, I blurted out the first thing that popped into my head. "Sorry to bother you, but my friend and I are lost." I shot June a smug glance because I had clearly saved the day, but the only thanks I got from my friend was a critical sigh and an eye roll.

The woman's clear blue eyes bore into mine as she removed one heavily ringed hand from her walker and placed it on her crooked hip. "How can you be lost? Didn't Pervis just drop you off in front of my house? I'd know his clunky green van anywhere."

Oops. I wracked my brain for a logical explanation and hoped I could come up with something because I was certain we wouldn't be getting a third chance. "I meant we've lost our friend. We aren't lost, but we were supposed to meet up with our friend Zach, and now we can't find him. Pervis has been sort of our tour guide today, and it turns out he knows Zach. He said he comes here sometimes, so we thought it couldn't hurt to stop and see if he was here or if you had seen him tonight."

I held my breath and crossed my fingers while Ms. Conner considered my words and continued to look us up and down. Finally, she shuffled out of the doorway and invited us to come inside. I could tell June was surprised we achieved our goal by simply knocking on the door and telling the truth. Well, almost the truth.

We followed our hostess into a tidy living room that smelled of cinnamon and old books.

"Can I offer you girls a cup of tea? I was just about to pour one for myself."

"Don't go through any trouble," June said. "That would be lovely," I said at the same time.

Ms. Conner retrieved two more teacups from a well-stocked curio cabinet and placed them beside her own on a tray. The lavender china teapot she poured from looked about as old as our hostess.

"What did you say your names were?" she asked, once the tea things were properly arranged on the coffee table.

"My name is Francie, and this is my friend June."

"There's no need to shout, dear. I'm old, not deaf."

"I'm so sorry, ma'am," I said, trying to modulate my voice.

She picked up her teacup, moved it to an end table, and twisted the onyx ring on her index finger before settling herself in an overstuffed chair upholstered in faded velvet cabbage roses. When she had settled in, she waved us toward the sofa. "Sit, please, and let's start over from the beginning. Why are you really here?"

So much for patting myself on the back for my brilliance. I felt like I was sitting in the principal's office about to be scolded. I wasn't too far off.

June cleared her throat and tried to salvage my not-so-impressive first impression. "Ms. Conner..."

"If you already know my last name, you might as well call me by my first. It's Bea."

"Thank you, Bea," June continued. "I apologize for getting off on the wrong foot. We were afraid you wouldn't agree to speak to us, and didn't want to intrude."

"But you did anyway."

Yikes. If I hadn't detected the twinkle in her eye, I would have bolted out the door, but I got the impression Ms. Bea Conner was enjoying herself at our expense. I guess being the evening's entertainment was preferable to being hauled off to the police station for harassment.

June was good at reading people too, so I sat back and watched as she turned up the charm. "I'm a reporter out of Cleveland, and I'm here on the island working on a special news story. It started out as a colorful piece on Pirate Fest but has developed into a more serious story about island history. Zach mentioned you had a unique perspective—especially about the Hotel Victory and the fire that destroyed it. I was wondering if you'd be willing to share some of your knowledge with me."

Bea's blue eyes lit up. "Oh, yes, dear. I'm always happy to get the word out about our wonderful town, especially to the younger generation. There's so much more to the island than drinking and carrying on, you know."

June nodded her head in hearty agreement. I could relax. It was plain to see we had made a new friend.

Our hostess sipped her tea and continued. "Zach asked a lot of questions about the fire too. He also offered to help me catalog the volumes of books, photos, newspapers, and the rest of the memorabilia, so it could be archived online. The historical society has limited resources as far as technology goes, but Zach was putting in hours going through all this stuff and using his own software to sort it all out. What a dear young man. And he did it all for free. He wouldn't even let me introduce him to the board of directors so he could at least receive credit for all his help."

I wondered what he was up to. Was he really the helpful young researcher Ms. Conner thought he was, or was he looking for something specific—a treasure map perhaps, or another clue pointing to the location of some lost pirate bounty?

I continued to puzzle over my questions as we sipped our chamomile tea with honey and lemon and listened to Ms. Conner's stories. She told us about her mother and her best friend, Hazel, who worked at the Hotel Victory during its heyday. We learned about other smart, innovative people who lived and worked here over the past two centuries. Once she got started, I saw Bea would have been content to talk through the night. It was getting easier to imagine Zach had visited Ms. Conner again and again for the simple pleasure of listening to her stories and helping her preserve and organize them for future generations.

I was enjoying this cozy respite from the crazy day we'd had. Whether or not anything we learned from our visit to Bea Conner would end up helping us figure out who was behind Chef Truffle's untimely demise remained to be seen.

Chapter 16

I stretched myself awake and was happy to see I'd slept until nearly eight o'clock. June wasn't in bed, and I heard nothing from behind the bathroom door, but before I had time to get anxious, I spotted the note on the bedside table. *I'm rounding up some breakfast. BRB. Make coffee!*

I hummed a few show tunes as I got myself around. Thinking about last night's visit with Bea Conner made me smile. She was an island treasure who was willing to share her wealth. I hoped Zach's intentions were honorable, but how could I know for sure?

It felt good to engage in the simple ritual of making morning coffee—almost normal. I was pouring a second cup when June returned, balancing a white bag in each hand and a newspaper under her arm. She plopped the provisions on the dresser, poured herself a mug of coffee, and settled in with her newspaper.

After flipping through the pages, she stopped at a section near the back and read for a while, pausing occasionally to direct her attention to her breakfast sandwich. "Look here. I found the obituary notice for Theodore Truffle." She pushed the paper across the table so I could read it. "It mentions his mother in Columbus and also a half brother. The brother's name isn't listed, and there's nothing else about him included."

"That's unusual isn't it?"

"Not as unusual as you might think. This is a very small town with a matching budget. The staff writer who put this together probably didn't give it much thought."

"So, Truffle was not married and had no children. His only survivors are his mother and brother. Do you think he had a big insurance policy or something?"

"That doesn't feel right. If it was insurance money someone was after, they'd have tried to make his death look like an accident."

"Right. And we both know there was nothing about the scene that remotely resembled an accidental death. It looked more like a crime of passion or anger. What could Truffle have possessed to cause such a violent act?"

June folded the paper and set it down. "Solving a puzzle like this is much harder than deciphering clues in a scavenger hunt, but we can't get discouraged. Every tiny piece of information gets us one step closer to the truth."

"Being a reporter and being a detective have a lot in common, don't they?" I thought about how June and Lucas Rains not only made an attractive couple, but also how their personalities and jobs were seeming more and more compatible. Of course, the same could be said about her and Detective Jack Morgan. I was glad I wasn't the one having to sort through all those feelings.

"At least we don't have to work on an empty stomach. I was a lot hungrier than I realized until you provided breakfast. How did you manage to pull this one off?"

"I ran into that nice cabin boy on my way to the galley. I told him I was your guest and you were feeling under the weather. He offered to put together a to-go breakfast for both of us which I thought was very nice. While I was waiting in the hall, Captain Blackhart showed up."

I washed down my egg and bacon croissant with the last of my brew. "This is delicious. I'll have to remember to give him a nice tip when I finally get some cash. Did you say you ran into Blackhart? What did our illustrious captain have to say? Did he ask you out?"

"No, no. But he did ask what happened to us last night. He was concerned about you, and when I left before dinner and never returned, he sent someone to look for us. He said he eventually learned we were back aboard the ship, so he didn't disturb us last night."

"Just as well. I wouldn't have had anything to tell him. I think I need to turn these wallets in to him though. Maybe he can help get them back to their owners."

"Should we let Lucas have a look first? He did say to call him with any updates."

"So, it's Lucas again, is it?" June's cheeks were pink.

I toned down the teasing and admitted that informing Lucas wasn't a bad idea. "Go ahead and call him while I get dressed. He can decide what to do with them. There's no driver's licenses or money in any of them. There are a few loyalty cards and some other papers though. I'm sure someone can track down the owners and get their belongings back to them. I can't remember anything about how I got them and that scares the heck out of me. The sooner they're out of here, the better."

When I emerged from the bathroom, June was saying goodbye to Detective Rains, aka Lucas. She informed me he told her to go ahead and leave the wallets with Blackhart, but to be sure to let the captain know he'd be by to take a look at them later this morning.

"Okay, that makes sense." I grabbed the plastic bag that would be doing double duty as my handbag for the day, tossed the four wallets and the sunglasses inside, fluffed my hair, and headed for the door.

Blackhart was gracious when I handed over the wallets, assuring me he'd turn them over to the authorities as soon as he checked the names against his lost and found record. I did a good job evading most of his questions about last night's episode and left his cabin feeling satisfied we'd done the right thing. Before I could strain my arm patting myself on the back, June grabbed me and shoved me into a nearby doorway.

"What the...?"

My question was answered before I finished asking it. Liz Fuller was heading for the captain's quarters carrying two, no, make that three, wallets. As soon as the door closed behind her, we tiptoed back and pressed our ears to the door. Voices traveled surprisingly well, and we had no difficulty eavesdropping. Liz was explaining to Captain Blackhart how she had found some empty wallets and wanted to turn them in to the lost and found. I wondered if she noticed the four similar billfolds likely still sitting on top of Blackhart's desk where he'd placed them seconds ago. As they were saying their goodbyes, we hightailed it back to the relative safety of our doorway alcove. From our hiding spot, we watched as the door opened. Liz looked happy and relaxed. She smiled at Blackhart when he blew her a kiss. Really? Wasn't she a little young for him? The helpful cabin boy led her out of the captain's quarters and walked her down the hall, guiding her by the elbow.

"Coincidence? I think not." I was in accord with June's observation.

"Whatever's going on around here, both Liz and the captain are involved. We need to keep an eye on those two."

"Yes," June said, "and that cabin boy sure gets around. We need to get started on the treasure hunt for the day, but I still think we need to keep our eyes on everyone involved in this convoluted production. And whatever happens, don't leave my side without telling me where you're going. We can't afford to have a repeat of last night. Stay on your toes, and let me know if you see or feel anything strange."

"Aye, aye." I saluted my friend. As I did, I had a flash of a memory. A singing fish? That couldn't be right. I started humming George Harrison tunes as we left the ship and headed to our golf cart.

I was relieved when June slid behind the wheel. Normally, it would have been my turn to drive, but I was still grounded. My hope was that by sitting back and taking in my surroundings, I might put some of the puzzle pieces together. Between talking birds, singing fish, and hot flashes, I needed time to sort out what was real and what was fantasy, and hopefully, sooner rather than later.

"Where to, Francie? Did you ever figure out the location of the mystery ship from the last clue?"

"If I did, it escapes me at the moment." I didn't mention I was trying to remember what a fish told me last night.

"Didn't you say something about a ship that never leaves the island?"

"I may have, but I was just thinking out loud. Can you think of one in particular that might be our next stop?"

June shook her head. "There's an old tug boat over at Miller Marina that never leaves the dock."

"I don't think that's it," I said.

"Probably not." June adjusted the rearview mirror, stalling for time.

"I've got it! I know what it is. Oh man, it's so obvious, it's embarrassing. My brain must be addled from whatever got to me last night. Let's go!"

We didn't move. June looked concerned. "Care to share your great epiphany, or am I supposed to read your mind?"

"Oopsie. I just got excited. A moment of perfect clarity is a beautiful thing."

"Once again, care to share?"

I took a deep breath and began. "Yes, of course. I'm certain the next stop on our treasure hunt is the Benson Ford Shiphouse. I'm sure you've seen it from the water. It juts out from the cliff on the back side of the island."

The Benson Ford was a landmark unlike any in the world. The original ship was built in 1924 by Henry Ford and named after his grandson. After fifty years of service on the Great Lakes, the ship was scheduled to be scrapped at the Port of Cleveland in 1986 when it was saved from obscurity by a husband and wife with a vision and the resources to carry it through.

It took a minute for June to make the connection. "Yes, of course. That makes sense. I forget about that place, because you can't see it from the road. I've never been there, have you?"

"No, but I've seen pictures of the front quarters that the owners had removed from the rest of the original ship and turned into a magnificent residence. It was designed by Henry Ford himself. The walnut-paneled state rooms, dining room, galley, and passenger lounge are all still in mint condition."

"Can you imagine what it cost to separate that whole section from the ship, have it relocated by barge, and then lifted up the side of a cliff?"

"Not in my world, but I heard they sometimes give home tours. I wonder if this weekend is one it's open to the public."

"I heard somewhere that Johnny Depp bought the place. Wouldn't that be cool? He's even cuter than Cole Blackhart."

I rolled my eyes. "I'm sure it's a rumor, and I think you've got your dance card pretty well filled up these days."

"Just sayin."

Now that we had a destination, we felt we could relax and come up with a strategy. We decided to take some time and get a handle on where the rest of the participants were headed. We were confident we were on the right track, but it wouldn't hurt to see where we stood with the competition. As June drove the golf cart in the general direction of the rocky cliffs on the backside of the island, we solidified our plan.

We pulled into the parking lot of Joe's Bar, just behind the sign proclaiming "You Found It!" Joe's is an out of the way establishment that doesn't do much marketing but always has a full house. It's not fancy, and its self-proclaimed title of "Best Dive Bar on the Planet" lets you know up-front they're proud of who they are. The building is an old press house where they used to press grapes and make wine. They have a stocked humidor and live entertainment, making it one of Hamm's favorite stops whenever we visit the island. Did I mention they make a killer Bloody Mary? All things considered, it was the perfect place to sit at a picnic table and watch the traffic go by. Anyone heading to the Benson Ship Residence would have to drive right past us.

"Grab us a table and I'll go inside and get two Bloody Mary's." June was already headed for the door.

Best friends do that. They read each other's minds. I picked a table in the morning sun with a clear view of the road. Before June was back with our breakfast drinks, Zach and Bradley zoomed by in their golf cart headed toward the cliffs. I once again had the sense they were somehow one step ahead of the rest of us and wondered how they managed it.

June pushed the door open with her hip, spotted me, and did a great job balancing a full glass in each hand without spilling a drop as she sat next to me. Handing over a glass brimming with colorful healthy vegetables, she lifted her breakfast drink in a toast.

"Here's to a successful day and a big win." I didn't even bother to ask her how she paid for the drinks. She was resourceful, and whatever she did it worked.

"Cheers to that. And may our successful day include my husband's arrival, good news about your boat, and cash."

We clinked our glasses a second time and settled in. I told June about seeing Zach and Bradley, and she agreed there wasn't much more we could do at the moment besides keeping a close eye on their whereabouts. We were munching our celery stalks and enjoying the warm sun and cool breeze when the mood was shattered by the shrill sound of argument. No surprise, Marla and her daughter were zigzagging through the gravel debating whether to stop at Joe's (please no) or continue down the road. They spun their golf cart in a circle, stopped, and then headed back the way they had come.

"I don't know what to think about those two. I can't help but wonder how Beth and I would do under the circumstances."

"Are you kidding me? There's no way you can compare yourself to those two. You guys like each other. Sometimes I'm a little jealous of the relationships you have with your kids."

"I'm sorry. You're right. I'm lucky they turned into such great people."

"I think it was more than luck," June replied, concentrating once more on the festive garnishes in her spicy cocktail.

I focused on my own beverage and finally speared one of the queen-sized bleu cheese- stuffed olives with my little plastic drink fork. I had the prize almost to my lips when a familiar flurry of rainbow feathers swooped past my face.

Seconds later, I stared at my empty fork, stunned and impressed at the same time.

"Boy, that is one fast bird. I wonder if he went to stealth bomber school."

June was laughing, but I noticed she had her hand strategically placed over the top of her glass.

"Follow the leader. Follow the leader."

"Looks like Pretty Boy missed you. He wants to play. Isn't that sweet?"

"No, it's not sweet. It's annoying."

I had to duck at his next fly-by and swat at him to avoid a head-on collision. "I'm not in the mood for parrot games. There's enough game-playing going on all around us. I don't need to match wits with a kamikaze feather duster."

"Follow the leader. Follow the leader." Pretty Boy was insistent.

"Don't look now, but there goes Captain Blackhart."

Of course, I looked. Blackhart drove past in a shiny black open-sided Jeep heading the same direction Zach and Bradley had gone.

Pretty Boy circled faster and squawked louder, "Follow the leader. Follow the leader."

"I give up." I finished off my drink and stood up. "I think we've gathered enough intel at this location. It's time to get this show on the road. Follow that pirate!"

Gravel flew as June punched the gas and pointed the golf cart in the direction of the cliffs. It was easy to keep a safe distance since Blackhart's sleek black vehicle probably traveled faster in neutral than ours did in drive. We were so far behind him we nearly missed seeing the sudden turn he took. I was more than curious to know why he had veered from the main road and entered the drive to the state park. We could no longer see his vehicle, but the thumping bass drums and flute music blaring from his stereo kept him on our radar. Whatever he was up to, he wasn't trying to hide his whereabouts.

An image flitted through my mind. I was on a muscled black stallion with the wind blowing through my hair as we galloped past the vineyards toward the cliffs at the edge of the island. Did the ghostly Rose love the kiss of the wind on her cheeks? Did she even own a horse? Was she a figment of my overactive imagination? Or something else? Past and present, ghosts and people, dreams and wakefulness, so many things were tumbling around in my head.

June took a hard left, and I was jolted back to the here and now. Gravel spit from the two wheels still in contact with the ground. I braced myself against the dashboard in time to prevent myself from flying out the side of the cart as we came to an abrupt halt.

"What the heck?" I rubbed my neck and peered down the tree-lined road in the direction of the thumping stereo music in the distance.

"I almost missed the turn. Sorry. The park entrance isn't marked very clearly."

"It's okay. My mind was wandering or I'd have warned you it's gotten pretty overgrown back here. The campground is at the end of the road through those trees. I wonder what Blackhart is up to now. He sure was in a hurry."

"Or maybe he's just out for a leisurely drive on this beautiful morning. It only seemed like he was whizzing along because we're going so slow."

"Whatever. I think I might have whiplash." I rubbed my neck again. "Quiet. Do you hear that?"

"Hear what? I don't hear anything."

"Quiet!"

"What's your deal, Francie? I'm not talking, and I don't hear anything."

"Exactly. It's quiet. Blackhart either turned off his stereo or else he's already gone. We better get moving if we want to find out what's going on."

June shot me a quizzical look before restarting the cart and heading down the snaking trails through the park. We passed cabins, jet-ski rentals, and a quaint bar for campers whose version of roughing it was air conditioning, designer drinks, and fine china. I had forgotten how beautiful this area was. Tall oaks and maples that had seen the island change from battle ground to exclusive, world-renowned destination, and finally, to casual island resort, provided shade and a gorgeous backdrop to the lake where the gray-blue water lapped at the sandy shore beneath the cliffs.

On this holiday weekend, colorful tents were scattered about in every clearing. It was still early, so not many campers had ventured out yet. The younger crowd typically stayed up late and slept in, opting for the casual economy and flexibility of the campgrounds. There wasn't a two-night minimum stay requirement like at the hotels in town; and even better, out here off the beaten-path, no one complained if you stayed up all night, made excessive noise, or overindulged. Been there. Done that.

Blackhart must have come this way. There weren't any secondary roads, so we chugged along past burnt out campfires and overturned folding chairs. Swimsuits and towels hung on tree branches and makeshift clothes lines—colorful flags bearing witness to yesterday's fun.

"There he is—up past the fenced-in clearing."

June slowed as we drove by a sign designating the area as a historical spot. "What is this place? I've never been back this far before."

"I've been here, but it was a long time ago. Pull up closer to that sign. I have a feeling we just stumbled upon the ruins of the Hotel Victory."

June stopped the golf cart in front of the marker. "You're right, Francie. How cool is that?" She pointed to the large cement slab behind the chain-link fence. "That's the bottom of the swimming pool. According to this marker, it's all that's left of the Natatorium from 1898—a co-ed swimming pool—very forward-thinking for the times."

"He's getting out of his car, June. Time to quit brushing up on your history."

She looked up in time to see Blackhart leave. "Now what?"

"Drive over to the bath house and park around back. We need to hoof it from here if we want to see what he's up to without getting caught."

Blackhart had parked at the edge of a campsite just beyond the ruins. He walked toward the four tents set up in a semi-circle around a makeshift fire pit. A few glowing orange embers, a pile of gray ash, and a few black chunks of spent firewood were all that remained of last night's campfire. Like the other sites, discarded clothing and towels were strewn about, and there were no signs of anyone awake. Blackhart checked his gold wristwatch and poked at the ground in a few places with the tip of his boot.

June and I had crept around the back of the public structure and had a clear line of sight now. Something about this place was bothering me. I rubbed my arms to ward off the tingly feeling creeping up my extremities. It wasn't my imagination, or poison oak. I realized what I was looking at, and it terrified me. The T-shirts and swimsuits hanging from their haphazard drying places were all the same. They were also familiar. The neon green shirts with the word *Mermaid* emblazoned across the front in bright blue and the black one-piece swimsuits edged in matching greens and blues belonged to the girls on my daughter Beth's swim team.

June's pocket was vibrating. I shot her a dire look. "Make it stop. We can't get caught. Something bad is going on here, and I'm afraid Beth might be in danger. This isn't about winning a treasure hunt anymore or even solving a murder."

June powered off her phone. "What's got you so spooked?"

Even as she asked, she zeroed in on the scene and it took her only seconds to put it all together. She had been to more than one of Beth's swim meets, and even if she hadn't, she's good at putting the pieces of a puzzle together. Her eyes grew wide with the realization of what she saw.

From our vantage point, we watched and waited, determined now more than ever to solve some part of this mystery. Blackhart seemed to be waiting for someone. He stood off to the side of the tents where he wouldn't be easily seen by an emerging camper. He stood still as a tree. His smoldering eyes scanned the campsite, taking in every detail. He looked out toward the road then down at his watch. Finally, he exhaled deeply and motioned toward someone behind one of the tents beckoning him or her to come forward.

When the newcomer stepped out of the shadows, June and I whispered in unison, "It's the cabin boy!"

Our eyes were glued to the scene as it unfolded. Blackhart and the boy exchanged a few words, and a leather sack was passed from the captain to the young man. With an affirmative nod, the kid walked to the center of the circle of tents and gave a sharp whistle. One by one, each girl from the swim team, eight of them including my own daughter, stumbled bleary-eyed from their tents and stood in a lopsided circle with the captain's lackey in the center. From our hiding place, I could see Beth and the other girls clearly, but could only make out the side of the boy's head. He spoke to them, and they all nodded their heads in agreement. Next, he held the leather bag open. One by one, the girls stepped forward and dropped something into the bag. None of them spoke. Their movements were jerky and unnatural. After delivering their offerings, they each stepped back into their places and stood with their arms at their sides, hands empty, fingers limp. The whole scene was something straight out of a Stephen King novel. It took every ounce of restraint to hold back my motherly urge to spring out and save Beth and her friends. But I didn't know what I was up against, and I wanted answers, so I clenched my fists, bit down on my knuckle, and watched. I felt June's hand on my shoulder, steady, reassuring, letting me know without speaking a word she was prepared to jump in and kick some pirate butt with me if the need arose.

I placed a hand over hers in gratitude. I couldn't keep silent any longer. "Did those look like wallets to you? Those looked like wallets to me," I whispered in my friend's ear.

June nodded, never taking her eyes off the group. After the last wallet had been dropped into the sack, the cabin boy walked from one girl to the next, blowing each of them a kiss. When he finished this bizarre ritual, he said a few more words and left the clearing. Beth and her teammates reentered their tents without acknowledging one another or giving any indication anything was amiss.

Captain Cole Blackhart checked his watch yet again, walked back to his Jeep, and drove away, while the cabin boy slunk into the trees and wandered off without a backward glance.

Chapter 17

"Come on, June. Whatever else is going on here, my first priority is to make sure Beth is okay. I'm sure you noticed the girls were under some kind of spell. If that black-hearted buccaneer drugged my daughter, there's going to be more than one dead pirate on this island."

"I'm right behind you, Francie. Let's do this."

I made a beeline for Beth's tent. When I raised the door flap, I found her sitting on her sleeping bag rubbing her eyes. My heart nearly broke at the sight of my daughter. She was an adult on the verge of becoming a lawyer, but at that moment, all I could see was my child and her vulnerability. I approached her slowly, unsure of what to expect.

Her roommate was rummaging through a duffle bag as if her life depended on finding whatever it was she was searching for. This was an impossible situation with no precedent. No amount of improvisation or even parenting prepared me for the scene in front of me.

I held my breath until Beth finally looked up and her face registered recognition. "Mom? What are you doing here? Is Dad here? Do you have any ibuprofen? My head hurts."

"Oh, sweetheart, I'm right here. I'm right here." I gave my little girl a big mama-bear hug and helped her to her feet. "Let's go outside. There's something we need to talk about."

The wild look in Beth's eyes made me add quickly, "Everything's fine, honey. Everything is going to be fine." I hoped my tight embrace reassured rather than alarmed her because I had no intention of letting her go. Once outside, I loosened my grip and turned Beth to face me so I could get a better look at her. There was no evidence of physical harm I could see, but after that first glimmer of recognition, she had gone quiet again.

While I tended to my daughter, June checked out the campsite. She walked the perimeter and checked the area around the campfire, snapping photos with her phone. I was thankful one of us was still connected. By now, I was confident she had placed a few calls. Detective Rains might scold us later for interfering, but there was no question it was time to let him in.

One by one, the other girls were emerging from their tents. Whatever was influencing their behavior, it was affecting them in various ways. Penny, a pretty blonde with bouncy curls and flushed cheeks, was squinting and shielding her eyes. Madison and Ava, the only other two I recognized, were becoming confrontational. A fourth girl was twirling in circles with her arms outstretched and singing "Under the Sea."

There seemed to be no pattern to the girls' strange behavior, so there was no way to predict what to expect or how long it might last. Since I was intent on staying with my daughter, until the police got here, it fell to June to move between the tents checking on the rest of the team.

I spoke softly to Beth, trying to ease her back without increasing her anxiety. I wanted nothing more than to make the connection between her swim team and the crew of the pirate ship, but it was slow going. Her memory seemed to be tangled up with fantasy. One minute she was lucid, and the next she was complaining about bright lights and needing to get back under water before her scales dried up.

The scary thing was I could relate to her actions. I knew firsthand how frustrating it was to wake up disoriented and unable to remember recent events. The idea that these strange symptoms were affecting people all over the island and seemed to be connected with the staff of the *Angel's Trumpet* was sinister and frightening. Was Chef Truffle involved, or had he been a victim? Were members of my own winner's circle part of the problem? The questions mounted exponentially, the answers not so much.

I stroked Beth's hair waiting for the right moment to question her more directly about Blackhart, the cabin boy, and the strange ritual I had witnessed. June continued her step-by-step investigation—stopping at each tent, inputting observations into her phone, and trying to connect with the more docile girls. I watched as she wedged herself out of the last tent on her second circuit around the camp. She wasn't even fully erect when a girl I didn't recognize shoved her to the ground, wailed like a banshee, and raced toward the smoldering campfire waving June's cell phone above her head. All my efforts at maintaining tranquility were lost in an instant.

"Give that back you little delinquent!" June didn't stay down long. She hurled her athletic body toward the zombie-turned-psycho and tackled her to the ground. The phone flew from her grasp and landed near my feet where Beth and I sat. My daughter didn't react to the commotion, and I didn't want to break the tenuous thread of her recollection, so I coaxed the phone toward me with my foot until I could reach it with my right hand, all the while continuing to stroke Beth's hair with my left, and speaking low comforting words into her ear.

When I finally retrieved it, I tossed it to my friend who had recovered from her tussle with the thief. She wasted no time tapping buttons and scrolling through notifications while her tormentor huffed off. I turned my attention back to Beth trying to keep my composure for her sake, all the while fighting my internal desire to destroy whomever or whatever had done this to my bright beautiful baby and her friends. I stayed by her side while June made her way through the campsite for the third time. Even after being attacked, she was focused and efficient, scrutinizing every detail of the scene. She popped in and out of the tents, talked to the girls who were cooperative trying to establish some trust, and swatted away the ones who tried to argue or fight. Every few minutes, I noticed her checking her phone, which she had tucked down the front of her shirt for safekeeping.

Beth and I had moved into the shade of a nearby tree. We were sitting face-to-face now, Indian style. Her hands were in mine, and she was looking around her, scanning the campsite through squinted eyes. Once, her gaze lingered on my face. She tilted her head and her brow furrowed. "Mom?" It was as if she was seeing me for the first time. I grew increasingly alarmed, and had to remind myself I had June in this with me. I knew she had alerted the authorities and was sure she had expressed the need to get medical personnel out here as well. It was just a matter of time, but having no frame of reference, I couldn't dispel my anxiety.

It felt like Christmas morning when Beth's eyes lit up and a smile spread across her face. I wanted to jump for joy but reeled in my enthusiasm and waited for her next move.

"Daddy? Ben!"

My hopes were dashed. Beth was still confused.

"Hi, Sweetie."

Wait. What? I recognized that voice. Were her hallucinations contagious now? Strong arms encircled me from behind. A rough cheek brushing against my face and the familiar smell of Hamm's soap assured me this was not a hallucination. A tear leaked from the corner of my eye. The cavalry had arrived. It was okay for me to collapse now.

But Ben? What was he doing here? Beth's twin brother had made his way to his sister's side. Had June discovered some horrible truth and called the family? That didn't make sense. Even if it were true, there wouldn't have been time. Ben was supposed to be out of the country.

He gave his twin sister a gentle hug, said "Hey Sis," and sat beside her without another word. That bond you hear about between twins—it's real and it's powerful. I could feel the tension leaving her body. Family, done right, is a beautiful thing. The four of us sat still for a moment—connected and protected from the outside world.

Absorbing strength from my husband's touch and the knowledge we were all together, I got my act together. "What are you doing here Ben?" As delighted as I was to see my son, his unexpected appearance ruffled me. "Did you tell us you would be home this weekend?" There's no way I would have failed to remember my son's homecoming. I hadn't seen him all summer.

Never letting go of his sister's hand, Ben explained that his host had received an unexpected family visitor who would be staying on for a while, so he completed his commitment to the Peace Corps two weeks early and decided to surprise us for our anniversary. He went to Beacon Pointe, but it was only after he'd gone aboard our boat he remembered we'd be at Put-in-Bay for the pirate festivities and recipe awards.

"I was confused because no one was around and the boat was still at the marina. I talked to some of your friends, and they told me all about the nasty pump-out incident. Someone said security had been called because they thought I was an intruder. I guess it's a good thing people look out for each other on the dock, but I was a little ticked off because I'd have to stick around and explain myself to avoid being the target of a full-blown manhunt."

Hamm picked up the story from there and filled in the blanks. "While security was questioning Ben and verifying his identity, I showed up. I confirmed he really was our son, and he had permission to be on the boat. I think the security guard was disappointed there was nothing shady going on. He looked sad when he left. I figured Ben and I should take the morning ferry over and surprise both of you. I kept trying to call June's phone, but it went to voicemail every time."

I squeezed my husband's hand as he continued his story. I didn't realize how scared I was until I was allowed to let my guard down.

"When June finally responded to my calls and texts, you can imagine how worried I was. We came straight here to the campground. I'm surprised we got here before the cops. Any word yet on what this is all about?"

Hamm stopped talking and took a long look around starting with Beth and me. When he was satisfied neither of us was in any immediate danger, he stood and took in our surroundings. Most of the girls were quiet now. Some had gone back inside the tents. Two were walking in circles with their arms around each other's waists. Beth laid her head on Ben's shoulder, and he stroked her hand.

"First things first," my knight in shining armor announced. "We need to get a doctor out here to check on these girls. Something is very wrong, and although based on the way June said they were acting earlier, their symptoms are lessening. I'm worried that the cause may be hard to determine, and the longer we wait, the more difficult it will be to identify the source."

"I'll call 911 and get someone out here right away," Ben volunteered.

"I think we need to inform the police as well."

"Already on it," June said. "I called the police shortly after we got here and have been in contact several times already. In fact, I just got off the phone with Lucas. He's on his way here right now, and he's sent some officers to the *Angel's Trumpet* to have a word with Captain Blackhart and his cabin boy."

For the first time in a long while, I felt like I could breathe again. Beth was almost back to her old self, and thanks mostly to June's take-charge, no-nonsense responses, the immediate danger had passed, and others would be here soon to gather up the evidence and take care of the rest of the victims. An idea had been percolating in the back of mind, and now that I could afford to give it some time and space, it bubbled up to the front.

"Hamm, I'm so relieved you're here, and I can't believe Ben came home. He must be exhausted, and getting all the way here just to find himself in the middle of this crazy mess is the last thing he needs."

"It's probably the best thing for Beth, though. Look at the two of them."

I did. Hamm was right. They were two proverbial peas in a pod. Young, resilient peas, at that. Seeing them together gave me the confidence to do what I felt I needed to do next.

I pulled my husband aside and gave him the condensed version of what I had in mind. I knew he'd try to argue with me, which he did; and he knew once my mind was made up there'd be no chance of changing it, which there wasn't. When he was satisfied that I'd be careful, and that I might do more good than harm, he reluctantly agreed to let me go with the promise I'd keep him informed.

"Come on, June. We've got to hurry."

I kissed my husband and grabbed my best friend's hand, dragging her toward the public bathhouse where the golf cart was parked.

"Francie, have you lost your mind? Where are we going? Shouldn't we wait for Lucas and the doctors?"

"Shush. They'll be fine. Hamm's got it."

June, like Hamm, knew there was no point in arguing, especially since she didn't know what she was arguing about. It was my turn to take charge. I crossed my fingers and toes and jumped into the passenger seat. The race was on.

Chapter 18

Once we were in the golf cart, and June had the key in the ignition, she turned to me and scrutinized my face. "If I didn't know better, I'd say you've been bitten by whatever bug got to Beth and the girls. Come to think of it, you have been acting strange lately. Should I be worried?"

"Yes," I answered, "you should. If I'm right, we've been dancing around in the middle of this horrible scheme since the first day we arrived. Please just drive this tin can to the cliffs as fast as you can."

Satisfied that I wasn't completely out of my mind, June did as I asked. On the way, I filled her in on my ideas. She listened attentively and added some thoughts of her own. By the time we arrived at the rocky outcroppings on the backside of the island, we had formulated a pretty solid theory. That's not to say we'd come up with a solid plan for what to do about it all, but it was a start.

I recognized Zach and Bradley's golf cart parked near the entrance to the Benson Ford Ship Residence. June pulled in beside it, and cut the engine. "Here we are. Now what?"

"The police can only be in one place at a time, and right now they're needed most at the campsite, so we're going to find the rest of our shipmates and sort this out. They each have a piece of the puzzle, and if we work together, I think we can solve this thing."

"Like the treasure hunt!"

"No! The exact opposite of the treasure hunt. The treasure hunt is a competition. Everyone wants to be one step ahead of everyone else, keeping secrets and racing to grab up the clues and prizes. There's so much more at stake here. Chef Truffle is dead, the campsite is being used for some bizarre mind-control cult that requires wallet donations in the collection basket, not to mention I've had my own share of physical and emotional irregularities, and right smack in the middle of it all is the handsome, charismatic Captain Cole Blackhart."

"Okay."

"Okay? That's it? That's all you've got?"

"Well, you pretty much covered it all in that speech. You don't have to convince me."

"Oh."

"I guess there is one more thing. I can probably cross Captain Blackhart off my dance card for the time being."

"Phew. That's got to be a huge relief." June didn't take offense to my snarky comment. Like her own, it was a coping mechanism—a way to let off steam. Instead, she smiled, tucked the golf cart key in her pocket, and said, "Come on, partner. Let's do this!"

What greeted us as we made our way to the back of the lot was a scene I'll never be able to erase from my memory. Everything looked perfectly normal until we rounded the corner of the ship-turned-domicile. The lawn extended about forty feet where it met with the rocky ledge of the drop-off.

Zach and Bradley stood at the edge of the cliff facing away from us, arms extended like airplane wings. Behind them, close enough to whisper in their ears, stood Cole Blackhart.

The sight of the twin brothers hit me hard. Even from behind, they suddenly seemed so young and vulnerable. I thought of my own twins. "We need to get to them fast, and we need to call..."

By now, June had Detective Rains on speed dial. She held her phone up for me to see she already had him on the line. When she clicked off, she gave me the condensed version of their conversation.

"Some deputies and the doctor are at the campsite. The doctor is going to run a few tests on the girls when he gets them back to the clinic but says there's no permanent damage as far as he can tell right now. They haven't found the cabin boy yet, and Lucas was looking for Blackhart. Now that he knows where he is, he'll be here as soon as he can to pick him up."

"That's all good news, but I don't think we can wait. Who knows what he's saying to those poor boys. We need to stop him before something terrible happens."

We crept forward, aware that with every movement we could be discovered. There was nothing we could do to conceal our presence, so we had to concentrate on making no sudden movements or sounds to attract attention. After what seemed like hours, I was close enough to Blackhart to reach out and touch his ankle. I stopped breathing. I could now hear the soft words he was repeating in a hypnotic voice. He was so focused I don't think he would have noticed us if we had stood up and started doing jumping jacks.

"Take the leap. You can fly. Peter Pan will never die. Be a legend. Catch your fame. The prize is yours. You'll win the game."

I motioned June to come closer so she could hear too. Blackhart repeated the same phrase never raising his voice or changing his inflection. No one moved.

We exchanged knowing looks, and then all hell broke loose. At exactly the same moment, we lunged forward, each grabbing an ankle and yanking back, effectively knocking Blackhart to the ground face-first. When he stopped talking, it must have broken whatever bizarre spell Zach and Bradley had fallen under. They both dropped their arms to their sides and stepped back away from the edge of the cliff. They did not however aid us in our tussle with the captain. We were all arms and legs and ninja moves, throwing in some screaming and shouting for good measure. I grabbed at anything and everything I could find to throw at or smack the pirate.

We lost the upper hand as the element of surprise wore off and Blackhart turned his full attention to his manic attackers. Although there were two of us and only one of him, he was bigger and stronger. Blackhart's boot connected with my body and I gasped in pain. Grabbing my side, I managed to roll away. June was on Blackhart's back, her arms around his neck and her legs wrapped tightly around his waist. He tried to fling her off, but she was stuck like a monkey on a tree branch.

I tried to stand but my knees buckled. Every intake of breath sent knife pains through my chest. I didn't need an x-ray to tell me I had at least one broken rib. Blinking away tears, I watched June and Blackhart spin and flail in a deranged dance and wondered how long it could go on before one or both of them went over the cliff.

Unable to help June in the fight, I looked around trying to find a rock or stick I could aim at Blackhart's head. All I found was a newspaper on the grass near my foot. It was the same one I had stashed in my grocery bag purse earlier. I snatched the paper and rolled it into a makeshift bat. As worthless a weapon as it was, it was all I had.

Gingerly, I got to my knees. Blackhart had broken free from June's vice-like embrace and was steadying himself. June wasn't backing down. I heard footsteps crashing behind me, and prayed they belonged to Lucas Rains.

The pain in my rib cage was not letting up. I swiped my hand across my face to clear my vision and saw what I thought was a flash of jet-black hair with a white streak. "Marla, help! Blackhart's gone crazy!" I yelled.

Marla whizzed right past me, blowing a cloud of dust into my face as she headed straight for June. "Goodnight, losers," I heard her hiss as a puff of dust left her hand and hit June smack in the face.

My brave friend slumped to the ground, her fists still poised defensively under her chin. I lowered myself back to the grass, lying still, taking my cue from June who was staring at nothing and making no effort to get up.

Captain Blackhart shook both his hands and brushed off his pant legs. Regaining his composure, he caught Marla in his fierce gaze. "Where have you been?" I heard him ask. I couldn't make out her reply. Remaining motionless, I moved my eyeballs trying to assess the situation without letting on that I hadn't joined the ranks of my powerless shipmates. June still hadn't moved. Zach and Bradley were safely away from the edge of the cliff but looked listless and confused. They made no attempt to confront the captain or Marla or to assist June or me. The only guest from the *Angel's Trumpet* unaccounted for was Liz Fuller. Lord only knew where she was or what she was up to.

Now what? I couldn't just lie here waiting for the next catastrophe to hit me in the face, but what else could I do without bringing the wrath of the crazy captain back down upon my friends and me? Surely Rains would be here any second.

Blackhart spoke urgently to Marla with his hands planted firmly on her shoulders. I ventured a glance in the direction of the house and thought I saw a slight movement among the trees lining the gravel drive. I didn't imagine it. There he was—the mysterious man who had a special talent for showing up when he was needed most. Michael's eyes met mine, and he raised a finger to his lips in a gesture I understood immediately.

"*Verfolgungsjagd*!"

And just like that Gunner leapt from the cover of the trees and pounced on Marla. The sight of the handsome shepherd sparked something in June. She propped herself up on her elbows and looked around. It was obvious, even to her confused mind, things were not as they should be.

"Francie, what's going on? Why are we on the ground? What's Gunner doing on top of Marla Fuller?"

"Try not to make any sudden moves, June. We don't want the captain coming over here. Marla blew something in your face and you collapsed. I held my breath at the last minute, so it didn't affect me. They don't know that though. It might be the only thing we have going for us at the moment."

Marla was whimpering and begging Gunner not to eat her. Gunner remained on full alert with his paws on Marla's shoulders, pinning her to the ground, but he didn't seem at all interested in making a snack out of her. Blackhart seemed unsure of what to do next. He wasn't moving to help Marla. He either didn't care what became of her or didn't want Gunner's attention shifted toward him. Zach and Bradley were behind him, slowly but surely advancing in his direction. June and I were stretched out on the lawn. I hoped he thought we posed no immediate threat. The whole scene was a strange tableau reminding me of Freeze Tag, a game I played as a child, where the goal of the person who was "it" was to catch the rest of the players and freeze them in their tracks. Unfortunately, this was no game, and Blackhart's uncertainty was short-lived. Before he spun around, I caught a strange glassiness in his eyes.

Arms outstretched, he pointed at Zach and Bradley simultaneously. "Down, boys!" he commanded. His voice was low, but there was no question of authority in it. Both guys stopped moving toward him and slumped to sitting positions. Once he was sure they were down and in submissive positions, he turned his attention toward June and me. I reached for my friend's hand and squeezed, afraid for both of us and unsure of how June might react. People, including me, were behaving in all manner of bizarre ways lately, and there was no telling if they would be docile or aggressive. June grinned at me, squeezed my hand in return, and said, "Isn't this fun?'

Before I could figure out how to reply, a motorcycle roared up the gravel path effectively capturing everyone's attention.

Detective Lucas Rains cut the engine and stepped off the bike. The gun in his hand spoke louder than words, and Blackhart raised his hands in submission.

Rains took stock of the scene. He tilted his head, stared out toward the trees, and nodded decisively. I heard a familiar whistle, and Gunner backed away from Marla, looked toward the sound, and bounded back to his waiting master. I was sure there would be a reward for the dog's brave actions. I offered up a silent thank you for Michael's role in our safety and vowed to thank him in person when this was over.

Rains returned his full attention to his pirate prisoner. "Well, Blackhart, you have a lot of explaining to do. But first, if you don't mind, I have a set of silver bracelets I'd like to add to your jewelry collection. He held out the handcuffs and waited for Blackhart to offer his wrists. The satisfying click of the cuffs did much to assuage my anxiety.

I heard sirens in the distance heralding the arrival of law enforcement. Things were finally looking up. While we waited for backup, I filled Rains in on what I had witnessed. It was slow going, because the throbbing in my side made it hard to talk. Rains was patient and offered me two aspirins from a bottle he had in his pocket. I accepted them gratefully and swallowed them without water.

I told him about leaving the campsite and following our treasure hunt clue to the Benson Ford Ship Residence and how we found Zach and Bradley about to take flight off the edge of the cliff while Blackhart encouraged them. I admitted that until then, I had suspected Zach or maybe his brother was either responsible for Chef Truffle's demise, or at least heavily complicit in the murder.

I was still holding the rolled up newspaper I'd been planning to use as a weapon. When I offered it to Rains, he accepted it without comment. I'm sure he knew what the outcome would have been if I'd tried to use it against Blackhart. Rains unrolled the paper, and I saw it was still folded to the story about the stinky plant causing the local library to evacuate. My eyes lit up as I remembered why I had saved the paper in the first place.

"You have to read this story," I insisted, poking at the article.

He skimmed the story and handed the paper back to me looking like he was wondering where the nearest loony bin was and how quickly he could get me signed in.

"I know, right?" I said proudly.

"Francie, did Blackhart hit you in the head?"

"No, I'm fine." But as I said it, I grasped my side.

"You need to take it easy. The medics will be here soon to get you checked out. In the meantime, you may have this all figured out in your head, but I do not know what you're getting at. What could last month's Island News have to do with what's going on here or identifying Truffle's killer?"

I told him about the powder Marla had blown into June's face and how she tried to zap me too, but I realized in the nick of time what was going on. I brought up all the blowing of kisses I'd witnessed lately, but I still wasn't getting through to him, and I sensed he was tiring of my obtuse explanations.

The island police arrived, and Rains jumped at the chance to leave me to my musings and the medical staff who had arrived just behind them.

He stuffed Blackhart into the backseat of a patrol car. "Get this thieving crook out of my sight." He slammed the door shut, but before the officer headed back to town, the detective signaled him to stop the car. Rains reopened the door, and pulled Blackhart back outside. I watched as he patted him down, checked his pockets, and confiscated several items from him. This time the look he gave me was one of understanding.

When the car pulled away with Blackhart safely back inside minus a few of his possessions, Detective Rains helped June to her feet and led her solicitously to the waiting ambulance where my vitals had already been checked and my ribs wrapped nice and snug. Her face lit up when she saw me, and she turned to Rains with a goofy grin and said, "Isn't this fun?"

"Yes, June, it's a blast." He put a blanket around her shoulders and took a few steps back.

"Francie, stay here with June. I need to have a word with Mrs. Fuller."

"I'm not going anywhere," I said.

I sat next to June in the open doorway of the ambulance. Rains was having a serious conversation with Marla who was cooperating for the most part; although, she occasionally swatted at the air around her head and glanced anxiously around. Rains flipped pages in his notebook and jotted additional info as he talked to her. Suddenly, I wondered where Liz was. I saw her this morning in Blackhart's office offering him the lost wallets and once more as she drove by with her mother in the golf cart. Did Marla drop her off somewhere? Was she working with Blackhart? Did she have information about Truffle's murder? Or worse? Perhaps she had been apprehended and was waiting for her mother at the police station.

Marla handed Rains an envelope, which he added to the items confiscated from Blackhart. The second patrol car waited, engine running, back door open, until Rains settled her in with a gentler touch than he had used on Blackhart. With a slap on the hood, and a wave of his hand, he sent suspect number two off to be processed.

Zach and Bradley were being tended to by a medic who led them to a second ambulance. Between the spectacle at the campground and the odd assortment of patients and suspects at the current scene, I guessed this was the most excitement the rescue squad had seen in years.

I turned my attention back to my friend. "How ya doin', June?"

She smiled at me as the medic closed the ambulance doors for our ride back into town. "Isn't this fun?"

Chapter 19

Through the back window of the ambulance, I watched as we passed the local clinic that served the needs of the tourists, continued to the main street, and stopped in front of the marina where the *Angel's Trumpet* bobbed serenely at the dock, its snowy white sails fluttering in the peaceful breeze. We had come full circle. The driver parked and came around to assist us. June was showing signs of her old self. I stepped cautiously out of the ambulance, and once I established I was steady on my feet, assured the medic I could handle it from here. I took June's elbow and guided her toward the ship.

As we got closer, I could see the ship's deck was buzzing with activity. Medical-looking personnel scurried back and forth between girls I recognized from the campground, and I realized the vessel had been transformed into a makeshift recovery room. I looked more closely, and relief washed over me the minute I saw my whole family huddled in a tight circle near the main mast. Hamm was rubbing Beth's back, and Ben was holding her hand. I couldn't wait to join them.

As much as I was concerned about June, I was thankful when I saw Detective Rains pull up behind the ambulance on his motorcycle. There was a genuine look of concern on his face when he realized it was empty, but he figured out where we were, and I waited for him to catch up to us. He walked straight up to June, not even pretending he didn't have eyes only for her. He gave me a polite acknowledgement, and took over.

In seconds, he had her on board the ship and settled in a deck chair to wait her turn with a health professional. In return, she smiled sweetly at him and uttered, "Isn't this fun?"

I followed them onto the ship, happy that my best friend was in good hands because I was intent on one thing—reuniting with my family. After a few happy tears, lots of hugs, and reassurances from everyone, I let my guard down and relaxed for the first time since pulling up to the campsite. It seemed like an eternity ago. We compared stories and filled in the gaps trying to weave together a more complete explanation of the events of the past few days. We talked nonstop for over an hour during which time I kept an eye on June from across the deck. I wasn't the only one who had an eye on her. Lucas Rains had gotten right down to business, interrogating everyone aboard the vessel, but every few minutes he made his way over to June, offering her a drink of water, a bite to eat, or a word of encouragement. There was no denying they made a cute couple, but to be honest, I hoped this handsome detective would turn out to be a diversion for June. I had my hopes pinned on the other detective in her life.

At last I felt I had the strength to leave Hamm and the kids for a few minutes and check in with June and Rains. I was getting around better thanks to the aspirin, the bandage wrap, and the knowledge that all my loved ones were safe. I could tell June was feeling more like herself as she scrolled through her phone and bobbed her ankle up and down in spite of the goofy grin still on her face. She looked content so I thought I'd start with the detective.

Rains was sitting at a table set up near the heart of the portable medical center. Lucky for me, he was closing his notebook as I approached. "What's up, Francie?"

I was happy he sounded a little less tense now because I had a few questions for him. "I know you're busy, but I need to know. All of this island crime—was it really about nothing more than pickpocketing pirates using Datura to get their way?"

"Datura? What do you know about Datura?" For once, Rains looked impressed.

"I have a few skills of my own, Detective. I know you thought I was crazy when I shared the newspaper article about the stinky plant with you, but it got me thinking. I did extensive research while I was perfecting my pirate stew recipe. My mind works in circular patterns if you will. I know some people think I'm scattered, but there's a method to my madness."

"Go on. You've got my attention."

"Okay, then. The first thing I did when I decided to enter the recipe contest was look up the sponsor company and the prizes. I loved the name of this ship and did an Internet search on *Angel's Trumpet* to see if I could learn more about it. Instead, guess what popped up first? Datura. It's a species of poisonous flowering plants. They're known as angel's trumpets and are also sometimes called moonflowers. I found this information romantic and interesting but not crucial to my recipe plans, so I didn't think of it again until I read the stinky plant newspaper article."

"I see what you mean by circular patterns."

Even as I continued my story, facts in my memory were clicking into place. "Another story I read up on and got a little obsessed with was the one about the local mystery of hidden treasure and how a very brave lady named Rose saved her family from marauding pirates. Guess what the name of their ship was?" I didn't give him time to ponder. "Yep, you got it. It was the *Moonflower*. Are you seeing a trend here yet?"

Rains whipped out his notebook and began flipping pages. Once he found his spot and had his pen ready, he asked me to continue.

"I looked into Datura a bit, but again, it wasn't my main interest. I'm sure any of these medical people around here could give you more complete information on the clinical details."

Rains didn't waste any time. He flagged down the first medic he saw. After a brief conversation, the young woman hurried off to help the handsome detective with some research. I shared the rest of my thoughts with him while we waited, including my dreams involving pirate activity. They seemed more sinister now than when I was anticipating my exciting prize weekend. It felt good to verbalize all my random thoughts and start to make some organized sense of it all. Maybe I should buy a notebook.

Rains clicked his pen as he listened, but his eyes never left mine. "We don't have a conclusive diagnosis on what's happened to all these people, but I agree you're onto something. You've been a big help, Francie."

The pretty young staff member returned and handed Rains several printed pages. "Here you go, Detective. My name is Carol. If there's anything else you need, don't hesitate to ask."

"There is one thing," Rains replied.

"Of course." Carol flashed a beautiful white smile and stood at the ready.

"Could you please see if there's anything you can do for the blond lady in the deck chair," he said, indicating June. I smiled and gave the detective a mental bonus point.

"Sure," she answered, a little less enthusiastically this time.

Since I was straining my neck trying to read the papers Carol had presented to Rains, he must have figured it would be easier on both of us if he just read them out loud. Score another point for Lucas Rains.

"Effects of Datura ingestion include a complete inability to differentiate reality from fantasy; hyperthermia; tachycardia; bizarre, and possibly violent behavior; and severe mydriasis (dilated pupils) with resultant painful photophobia that can last several days. Pronounced amnesia is another commonly reported effect."

"Wow. Someone must have been getting to us from the first day we got here."

"How's that?"

"Some of it I remember, but there's a lot that's happened I can't explain or don't recall. "I've been super sensitive to heat and light and have had some pretty strange encounters I'd rather not talk about right now."

Rains scanned the rest of the pages and handed them off to me before walking toward the knot of medical personnel poring over clipboards and talking in hushed tones. I rejoined

Hamm and the kids so I could read the rest of the report and share with them what I'd learned. I could count on them to help me make sense of my impressions. According to the report, victims of Datura poisoning typically required hospitalization. I felt a moment of panic, but as I looked around the deck, I realized none of those affected, including myself, seemed to have the degree of symptoms requiring stomach pumping or other drastic treatment. Maybe we were getting low doses. I still didn't know why, but I was developing a few theories.

A young man in scrubs approached us holding two syringes, a rubber tourniquet, and some bandages. It looked like those in charge with our recovery were getting on board with the Datura theory. Beth and I were about to give up some blood.

I saw June removing pressure from the gauze on her inner arm to accept a pill and some water in a paper cup. My guess was activated charcoal was being passed out to reduce the stomach's absorption of the poison. Both Zach and Bradley were wearing oxygen cannulas. Their symptoms were more severe than many of the others'. I sent up a quick prayer of thanksgiving that neither of them ended up at the bottom of the cliff, and that June, Beth, and I were not in too bad shape all things considered. I wondered if Marla was a victim too. Maybe she was acting under the influence of the drug. For her sake, I hoped so. And what about Liz? I needed to ask Rains if he knew where she was so I could stop worrying about her.

"May I have everyone's attention please?"

A familiar man in an expensive suit stood at the helm holding a microphone. His booming voice put a halt to all the chatter on the deck, and moved my fears about Liz to the back of my mind for now.

"Thank you all. My name is Parker Thorn, and I represent the Paradise Rum Company. As most of you know, this weekend was planned to honor three wonderful recipe creators and name the next spokesperson for our new marketing campaign. Unfortunately, events occurred, totally unrelated to our celebration or our company, that cut our plans short and resulted in all this."

He swept his hand in a grand gesture meant to take in all of us—poison victims, friends, family, medical staff, and law enforcement personnel—not the happy-go-lucky pirate party we had anticipated on our arrival. "According to the good doctors who have been working hard to diagnose and treat you, you will need to remain under observation until your symptoms resolve." He glanced at the paper he was holding and cleared his throat before continuing. "Which could take up to twenty-four hours."

He had to wait a beat for the murmuring to subside. "Be assured, all your medical expenses will be covered, along with meals and lodging. If there are special circumstances or additional needs, let one of my assistants know, and we'll make sure you're taken care of."

I scanned the deck and located the assistants. There were three of them, all dressed in the same black dress shirts and well-pressed black trousers, milling about among the patients, talking softly and exchanging information. When I had my turn, I was going to ask for someone to check on Liz since her mother wasn't around to worry about her.

Mr. Thorn spoke for a few more minutes, offering words of encouragement and repeating the part about none of this being the fault of the Paradise Rum Company. While he was speaking, a decent Jimmy Buffet cover band began playing in the background. The music increased in volume as Thorn made his final announcement. Everyone aboard the ship was invited to a deluxe barbeque being set up in DeRivera Park. I could see it from here.

Familiar island tunes began to soothe everyone's nerves with promises of wasting away in Margaritaville, and cheeseburgers in paradise. The tantalizing scent of grilling meat and an announcement of bottomless beers had most of the ship's current patients collecting their belongings and heading toward the sounds of rev erie without further coaxing.

As if Jimmy Buffet himself had broken through the last of the spell holding June hostage, she joined the rest of my family, humming and swaying her hips in time to the music. Hamm and I studied June and Beth for any symptoms of residual poisoning. When neither of us discovered anything more than off-key singing from our daughter and my best friend, I gave my husband the go-ahead nod to merge into the snaking line of people heading off the ship and into the park.

I couldn't believe it. All my loved ones were together and had no worries for the time being. Things were falling into place. It wasn't until I noticed the designer leather handbag slung over the shoulder of a departing guest that I remembered the problem that had loomed so large since my first day on the island. I felt suddenly naked. I squeezed Hamm's hand and nodded toward the woman with the enviable purse. Letting go of my husband, I grabbed June's hand and tugged her out of line.

"What are you doing, Francie? We were about to have endless BBQ and beers after three days of having to scavenge for our next snack. It was fun and challenging, but I'm not really up to it at the moment."

"I know. I just can't leave this ship one more time without my purse. You can clearly see the havoc its absence has caused so far."

"What are you suggesting? You're not planning to play pirate and pilfer a purse are you?"

"Of course not!" I could tell June was recovering. She was getting creative with her sentence structure again.

"Hamm brought one of my handbags from the boat when he came over today and left it in the room before he got your call and all hell broke loose. I just want to make a quick stop and grab it. Think of it as a security blanket."

"We could all use a security blanket about now. Let's do it and get ashore for some fun in the sun. Who knows, maybe we even won the treasure hunt. If everybody else was under Blackhart's spell, they might be disqualified from winning the prize."

"You have a point, June. But just a reminder, both of us have had our own moments of brain haze." I didn't want to think of the specifics. There were chunks of time I wondered if I'd ever get back. Worse still, I was pretty sure I didn't want to remember how certain things came into my possession, or what I may have done to acquire them.

"True, but we mostly used our powers for good. I'm optimistic. I think we still have a shot at first place."

She did sound cheerful, and I hoped it was her natural positive outlook coming through rather than any overlooked symptoms. I kept my pace just shy of a jog as we followed the hallway from the main deck down to the cabins since I wasn't up to full speed yet, and I wasn't sure if June was either. I shivered involuntarily as we once again rushed past the galley door with its painted parrot inlay on our way to the room June and I had been sharing in Hamm's absence. Fumbling, I put the key in the lock and shoved. Just as my husband had left a gold necklace and rose to surprise me on our first day aboard the ship, in the middle of the bed there now lay a worn leather shoulder bag bulging in spots from the treasures still inside. Hamm had chosen a familiar bag to make me forget about the one I lost. My eyes watered as I hefted it and peeked inside. For some women it's shoes or an expensive manicure, but for me it's always been the comfort of the perfect bag.

June leaned in the doorway smiling. At least she didn't mention how fun this was. I ducked into the bathroom to grab a tissue so I didn't look like a blubbering fool when we joined my family in the park. I was caught off balance when the room suddenly lurched to the right. There was nothing to grab in order to steady myself, so I was propelled forward, crashing into June and landing us both in a tangle of arms and legs on the floor. My chest flared with renewed pain reminding me all was not quite well.

"Is this ship moving?" June's head darted from side to side as she detangled her limbs from mine and pulled herself up to the room's porthole to see what was going on. I wrapped my arms around myself as tightly as I could and considered crawling under the bed to avoid the reality that we were in fact moving, and it was certainly not good news.

Chapter 20

"The ship is pulling away from the dock. I don't think that Thorn guy said anything about setting sail, did he?"

"No! This is not happening. Hurry up. We're getting off this tub right now. I don't care if we have to walk the plank to do it." Clutching my purse to my chest, I hauled myself up from the floor, wincing in pain, and headed for the door.

June followed close behind. "Um. How deep is the water in the harbor? Just a reminder—I can't swim."

"Don't worry," I said, trying not to worry. "We can't have gotten very far. Maybe the crew is just retying the lines or something.

We retraced our steps back to the deck. There were no crewmembers working on lines. In fact, the space was deserted. The only evidence there were ever people aboard the ship was some discarded paper cups, crumpled wrappers, and an assortment of empty chairs. My footsteps echoed in the empty space as I walked to the rail. People were lined up along the shore watching the beautiful *Angel's Trumpet* make its unscheduled departure. Some of them waved. Others looked confused, and a few, like my husband and children, looked frightened. I caught a glimpse of Detective Rains shouting into his phone as he ran toward the empty mooring, too late to retether a line or jump aboard. Captain Blackhart was supposed to be at the police station, so who was piloting the ship?

"Don't move!" a voice commanded from behind us. June and I immediately did the exact opposite, turning around to face our mystery skipper.

"I said not to move." The pirate repeated his order. At first glance, I thought Blackhart had returned, but it only took a second to realize it wasn't him. The man in front of us was much younger, and Blackhart's impressive wardrobe was baggy in the shoulders and droopy in the drawers on this imposter.

"Oh, hey," June's casual greeting belied the fact we were likely being taken hostage. "Aren't you the nice cabin boy we kept running into this weekend? You've been so helpful."

I poked her in the ribs. June had apparently forgotten the lad's sinister actions at the campground. Her recovery from the Datura was obviously not yet total. I kept my mouth shut so as not to aggravate the situation until I could figure out what his intentions were. I didn't see a gun, but that didn't mean he didn't have one. I was even more wary of the possibility he was concealing some of the mind-altering powder we were trying so hard to get out of our systems.

"Shut up and let me think."

This time, we did as we were told, but after a few minutes, I could hold my tongue no longer. I realized there was no one at the ship's wheel, and we were drifting dangerously close to the breakwall.

"Excuse me, Captain, sir, but don't you think someone should change our course so we don't smash into that wall?"

"You do it! Get over there right now and take us to open water. I can't drive this thing. I'm a cabin boy."

This news did nothing to assuage my growing concerns. Considering the options, I made my way cautiously to the helm station, not mentioning I was no skipper myself. I could tie a nautical knot with the best sailor and even drive our sedan cruiser out in the lake if Hamm gave me a specific heading and there were no other boats in sight. I was certain, however, I didn't have the skills to maneuver a giant schooner through a channel full of vessels of every kind while avoiding the solid steel breakwall that protected the harbor.

June decided it was time she said something as well. She approached the young man and addressed him fearlessly. "What's your name, cabin boy? I don't think you thought this plan of yours through, now did you?"

I was going crazy trying to figure out whether June was playing mind games with our captor or if her mind was playing games with her. Someone around here needed to take charge, and by the looks of it, that someone was going to have to be me.

First things first. I had no intention of going down with this ship, so I took a deep breath, channeled all my energy, grabbed the wheel, and turned it hard. A boat doesn't respond to steering the way a car does. It has a delayed reaction, so I feared the worst but hoped for the best. I thanked the gods of the lake and all the saints I learned about in elementary school when we narrowly avoided a collision the island would not soon have forgotten.

I was busy wiping sweat from my eyes and forehead, so it took an extra minute to notice there was now a fourth person on deck with us. A girl with long dark hair and sad dark eyes stood motionless at the door leading from below deck to topside.

"There you are, darling! Don't be shy. Come join me." The girl shuffled forward and stopped next to the cabin boy who drew her to his side. When the sun hit the girl's face, I recognized her immediately. Relief washed over me just before fear had the chance to wipe it away. Knowing Liz Fuller was alive and well was a comfort, but seeing her in this condition made all the crazy come crashing down around me in living color.

"Elisabeth, darling, come say hello to our new crew. I thought it was going to be just the two of us, but this is even better. We need people to take care of the ship while we concentrate on planning for our future. We'll get the answers we need and the treasure that is rightfully mine. All we need now is for you my darling to give me what Teddy gave you. Are you ready to share?"

Liz's expression never changed. What answers was the cabin boy talking about? What did he expect her to share?

The boy's face grew dark. His hold on Liz's arm was so tight it made me wince, but she didn't move a muscle.

"Where is it?" His gruff voice sent a shiver down my spine. His face contorted into an ugly mask. He screamed. "Where is it?" Although his mouth was practically touching Liz's ear, her face remained slack. Her vacant eyes scared me more than any look of terror could have.

June dove for the cabin boy's ankles and tackled him to the deck. That move was becoming more commonplace than I'd like to admit. Commonplace but impressive, nonetheless, especially considering June's diminished capacity. The counterfeit captain's voice rang with rage as he twisted toward Liz, flailing his arms intent on keeping his clutch on her secure. "Where is it, you bitch? Tell me right now, or I swear I'll kill you!"

The sailboat was bobbing gently. The sunlight sparkled on the surface of the lake. From the shore, the scene must have looked like an ad for the perfect summer getaway. But up close things were the opposite of ideal. It was going to take every ounce of determination and will to get us out of this.

I was the only one still standing. June's grip on the cabin boy was sure and strong. He had not released Liz's arm even after being brought down. She hit the deck beside them with a dull thud and stared into space.

"What have you done to this poor girl?" June demanded. She brushed off her knees, stood up and directed all the anger that had built up in her straight down into the cabin boy's face. "Let go of her, before I have to hurt you. I can and I will."

My friend was back. Maybe it was the adrenaline rush, or maybe the Datura had made its way out of her system. Whatever it was, I did a happy dance in my head. I no longer felt alone. We could do this.

I looked around for something I could use for leverage, but the deck was void of anything remotely close to weapon-worthy. I did the only thing left to do. I wound up and swung my handbag connecting with my target on my first try. The boy's head bounced off the teak deck with such a loud crack I feared I had killed him. He let out a low *Oof!* and let go of Liz, raising his hands to steady his wobbly head. He tried to sit up, but his eyes crossed, and he slumped back, eyes to the sky. June came up beside me and offered me a high-five. After a low five and a fist bump, we went to either side of Liz, helping her to her feet.

When she was steady, I asked June to stay with her and keep an eye on our crazy fake pirate while I went out to the bow to look for the anchor. With a pleasure I hadn't experienced in days, I rummaged through my handbag feeling for something we could use to keep our detainee in check. I wasn't disappointed. I found two pink bungee cords stashed in the bottom of my bag and tossed them to June who got to work wrapping them around the cabin boy's wrists and ankles.

"Keep an eye on this loser. I'll be right back." Even though the breeze was minimal, we were still afloat without anyone manning the sails or charting a course. I wanted to make sure when the rescue team arrived, they could get to us. If we drifted any further out into the harbor, things could get tricky. The area in front of the marina was full of boats tethered to mooring balls this weekend making it look like an overflow parking lot, which essentially it was. People aboard many of these boats were starting to notice us, and I'm sure concern was mounting. The *Angel's Trumpet* was not a vessel that could maneuver around or between any of them.

I was finally in my element. My purse was secured across my torso, and I was confident it wasn't going anywhere without me. I located the anchor locker on the bow, and steadying myself with the rail, flipped it open with my foot. The automatic winch pedal made it easy to lower the anchor with precision until it found purchase in the sand at the bottom of the lake. I breathed in the fresh air and breathed out a sigh of relief, feeling better than I had in days, in spite of my sore rib cage. In my mind, I saw Rose standing on the bow of a beautiful sailing vessel, but it was the *Compass Rose* not the *Angel's Trumpet* or the *Moonflower*. I was not Rose; I was Francesca. She was strong and beautiful, and best of all, she was she and I was me.

The sound of an outboard motor brought my moment of self-discovery to a close. A police skiff was approaching from the starboard side. I waved in greeting as I moved along the gunnel, keeping one hand on the rail. Near the stern, I found the rope ladder and lowered it. The cavalry had arrived once again and not a moment too soon.

Michael boarded first, followed by Lucas Rains. Gunner remained in the skiff, sitting at attention. It was easy to imagine the dog barking orders to a crew. Why not? If a parrot could help us solve a murder, a dog could be in command of a search and rescue team.

"Looks like you ladies have things under control here," Michael said, admiring June's handiwork with our prisoner's restraints. He continued his quick assessment, making his way around the perimeter of the ship, checking the hold of the anchor (it was fine, I might add), and finally heading below to make sure there were no more surprise interlopers aboard the vessel.

Lucas (I was finally convinced it was okay to be on a first-name basis with Detective Rains) asked about our safety, and when we assured him we were both fine, he turned his attention to Liz. He offered her a bottle of water and a small black pill. She swallowed the activated charcoal dutifully but made no attempt to speak. I hoped the neutralizer remedy kicked in soon so she could help us get a handle on what was going on here.

In the meantime, we had plenty to discuss. Lucas must have read my mind because the next thing out of his mouth was an assurance that Hamm and Ben were on shore with Beth and both of them had his direct phone number. They would remain in contact, and I could speak to my husband and kids very soon.

June was listening attentively. She was uncharacteristically quiet, and I knew this was because there was a black hole in her memory. I was aware how unsettling it felt for others to tell you about things you did and said, especially things like waking up in a bed of cake crumbs and talking to singing fish—things I would typically not forget.

"Lucas," I said, blushing only a little at the familiar use of his name, "Do you suspect Liz had anything to do with Chef Truffle's murder? I can't imagine a member of Beth's swim team could be involved in anything so diabolical, even with a mother like Marla Fuller."

Detective Rains pulled several photos from the inside pocket of his jacket and handed them to me. To my dismay, I recognized them as autopsy pictures. "Here's what we have so far. I'm hoping Liz can fill in some details when she comes around."

I forced myself to study the photographs one by one, handing each one to June before moving on to the next. "I didn't realize Truffle's tattoos were this extensive," I reflected.

"The ones on his arm were intricate and colorful; I didn't know they covered almost his entire body."

"Look at this one on his chest." Lucas pointed out a specific area on the photo in my hand.

"It looks like a map."

"It is a map—a map of a specific location right here on this island. See there? The place with the red X indicates the cliff where the Benson Ford Residence now stands."

He pointed out other locations on the human treasure map including the campground where the Hotel Victory once stood. I felt drained when I got to the last photo in the stack. It was a red heart located directly over Truffle's own heart. The initials HH were centered in the heart. A string of pearls encircled the heart. A teardrop hung from the bottom of the strand. It was beautiful and sad. I was sure this depiction was of something more than a simple pirate's lust. This artwork was personal and poignant.

"Wait a minute. Wait a minute." June stood and began to pace. Her investigative wheels were turning at full capacity. "Remember that article I found about Truffle's great grandmother, Hazel Henry?"

"Yes," I said, "she was working at the Hotel Victory when it burned down, right? She was an eyewitness willing to share her story. HH! Truffle's tattoo refers to Hazel, doesn't it?"

"Let me see that." Rains studied the photo with new eyes. "Let me get this straight. There's a connection between Truffle and some lost treasure? The murderer must have been trying to get the location of this treasure the night he was killed."

"I told him I didn't have it."

"What?" June, Lucas, and I all asked at once. We had been so engrossed in the photo of the heart and the treasure map, none of us noticed Liz was sitting up straight and alert, shuffling through the remainder of the pictures.

Her voice was soft and her eyes were wet as she said again, "I told him I didn't have it."

"Hey, Liz, you're back. How are you feeling? Do you want some water?" I was anxious to learn what she knew, but as a mother, my concern for her well-being trumped my new role as an amateur sleuth.

June's instincts were less mother and more reporter. "Who did you tell? What didn't you have? Did Blackhart kill Truffle? Did you kill Truffle? And what's up with this guy?"

June's last question focused all our attention back to the cabin boy-turned-pirate who was waking up from his involuntary afternoon nap. Michael had joined him, and I saw his pink bungee restraints had been replaced with metal police handcuffs.

Liz stared at the boy with new courage. "Levi? He wanted the treasure map. He said Teddy had the treasure map, and if I loved him I would get it for him and we could sail away to Barbados together. He said he loved me. I don't remember why I was leaving with him though. There wasn't any treasure map to give him. I sure don't love him; I mean I didn't even know his name until a few minutes ago.

"I knew Teddy though. He made me feel like I wasn't a freak hanging out with my mother on our first night here. He showed me his cool tattoos and even took me to his room and showed me a stack of family albums with pictures going back to his great grandmother. He talked about how she found some really expensive stuff in some guest rooms when that big hotel burned down, but how that wasn't the treasure. He said the real treasure was family. And love."

Her voice cracked at those last few words. I agreed one hundred percent with Theodore 'Teddy' Truffle. He may have looked like a linebacker, but the truth is, his name suited him. He was a big lovable teddy bear. At that moment I felt his loss profoundly and wished I'd had the chance to get to know him better.

"Where are my clothes?" Liz stared distastefully at her pirate wench ensemble. I put my arms around her shoulder and pulled her close. She was starting to shiver.

"It's okay, dear. I know this is very confusing right now, but you're safe. The pirates on this ship have been drugging us throughout the weekend to help them get away with all sorts of crimes. We're just starting to get the full scope of the enterprise. It seemed like Captain Blackhart was running this crew, but now it looks like this Levi fellow has the blackest heart of them all."

Chapter 21

We settled into our new temporary digs at the Island Resort Hotel. The guests of the *Angel's Trumpet* had been relocated to complimentary rooms for the remainder of the holiday weekend. We were allotted a premier suite so there'd be plenty of room for Beth, Ben, and June to bunk in with Hamm and me. Zach and Bradley were given adjoining rooms and the services of a private nurse to monitor their recovery from the Datura poisoning. Marla had been released from custody when it was proven she, like her daughter, had been poisoned and manipulated against her will. Both of them were also being watched closely for symptoms or complications of the drug. Whether it was due to higher metabolism rate or lower doses of the drug, Beth, June, and I were cleared by the medical staff and no longer required regular monitoring. That's not to say the men in our party weren't keeping watchdog eyes on our every move, which was completely fine with me.

The members of the swim team had been reunited with their families and brought to the mainland where they would receive additional medical attention and follow-up with a team of investigators helping to tie up loose ends in the case. The entire crew of the pirate ship was brought to the police station where, one by one, they were either exonerated or charged with various misdemeanors or crimes. Captain Blackhart and Levi the cabin boy remained in custody. I was anxious to hear if the official charges against them matched up with my own theories about their crimes, and now that June was feeling like herself again, she was making up for lost time pulling her breaking news story together—fact checking, finalizing her background research, and waiting to learn the official charges handed down to the two twisted transgressors.

"When do we get to eat?" It was Ben who asked out loud, but in this family, it could have been any one of us. We love to eat.

The phone on the bedside table rang, and I braced myself for bad news. I was having a hard time believing we might finally be through with murder and mayhem, so I took a deep breath and reminded myself what the medics had cautioned us about. It was likely I was suffering from a speck of residual paranoia from the Datura. Hamm picked up the phone, murmured a few assents, and hung up.

"Soups on, folks. We're meeting Lucas in the dining room, and he's going to fill us in on his investigation."

I exhaled. "Our investigation," I corrected Hamm.

"Yes, dear. I'm sorry. You had a big part in solving the case."

"Cases," June corrected.

"I'm going to be quiet now."

"Good call, Dad," Beth and Ben chimed in unison.

Lucas was waiting for us in the dining room. There was a round table already set for eight. "Will any of the others be joining us?" I asked, making note of the two extra chairs.

"I invited Marla and her daughter and the guys, but they all declined. All four of them are having off-and-on effects from the Datura, so they've been advised to lay low. Room service will be bringing their meals to them, but I kept two extra place settings just in case anyone changed their mind."

Appetizers and ice water were brought out and we all dug in with hearty appetites. I guess crime solving makes a person hungry. Although we kept the conversation light through the first course, I knew June had her iPad strategically stashed under the table. She wasn't about to waste a minute or chance missing any part of the exclusive scoop when it was delivered.

After the plates from our first course were cleared and we had placed our orders for entrees, the time felt right to do what we all came for. Lucas set down his fork, took a sip of water and started the ball rolling.

"Things didn't turn out as anyone expected, but it's been a weekend none of us are soon to forget."

"At least not on purpose," I added.

Hamm squeezed my hand under the table. He knew my lame attempt at humor was a coping mechanism just like June and I shared snide remarks and wisecracks when things got tough or uncomfortable.

Lucas was kind enough to humor me. June was riveted—either on what he was about to say or the way his eyes crinkled when he smiled.

"Okay, here's what we've got. Feel free to ask questions or add anything I might have left out." He paused briefly, looking at each of us in turn before starting his summary in earnest.

"Let's start with Captain Cole Blackhart." Images of the darkly handsome, romantic, larger-than-life figure I saw on my first day aboard the *Angel's Trumpet* morphed into a sinister predatory pirate in my mind. "Yes, let's," I agreed.

Hamm squeezed my hand again. I think this time it was a silent effort to get me to shut my mouth and let Lucas continue uninterrupted. I did.

"Yes, well, first of all, he really is a certified ship's captain."

June pulled out her iPad and began tapping without a word.

"Blackhart has been making a decent income hosting various exclusive events like the Paradise Rum Recipe contest for over ten years. He travels across the country playing his pirate role, and until recently has maintained a glowing reputation among high-paying clients."

"So what happened to plunge him into a life of crime?" This time it wasn't me, or even June. I squeezed my husband's hand to return the favor of a silent zip-your-lip alarm. "Sorry," he whispered between clenched teeth.

"I was going to save this part for later, but since you asked, it appears Blackhart got himself into some heavy gambling debt in the Caribbean. He was offered a way out by an unscrupulous organization that's been trying to establish a foothold in this part of the country. They're well known in Chicago, and I've been following them for years. That's one of the reasons I relocated to this area in April."

That reason happened to line up exactly with Jack Morgan's recent transfer from Chicago to the Erie islands, and was also the reason he was currently testifying in an important case back in the city.

I wondered about the other reasons, but kept my mouth shut. A man is entitled to his privacy.

"Anyway, the Scorpione family paid off his debt to the original creditors, but as you can probably guess, this favor came with a huge price tag."

"Wait. Did you say Scorpione? This is unbelievable! I thought if I never heard that name again it would be too soon." Everyone else at the table was nodding in vigorous agreement.

When Lucas mentioned the name, I had a flashback to the photo I saw in Blackhart's cabin of him and a beautiful woman with a scorpion tattoo. It must have been the Datura that caused me not to recognize Sirena Scorpione, the woman who nearly killed June and me and the same woman Jack was in Chicago testifying against. She had been younger in the photo, but under normal circumstances, I would have recognized her immediately.

"Blackhart fell deeper and deeper in debt to the family. He finally concocted a scheme to haul in the extra cash he needed to get out from under the mob and start accumulating a nice bank balance."

It was Beth's turn to ask a question. "Is that why he drugged me and my teammates? To steal money for him from tourists?"

"That's exactly right, Beth. Some of the crewmembers admitted to scouting groups of young people, especially at the campgrounds, who could be drugged and instructed to go into town at night and mingle with tourists in the bars. The suggestive powers of the drug are very strong and it causes memory loss on top of it. For a while, it was the perfect combination."

Beth looked horrified. "I don't remember anything about where I was that night. I can't even imagine picking someone's pocket, let alone getting away with it."

I thought about Liz Fuller in the boutique, and wondered how many wallets she had stolen without remembering. I'd be willing to bet June's was her first. And what about the empty wallets I found in the plastic bag under my bed? I shuddered to think where they had come from. The gaping hole in my memory would haunt me long after we returned home.

June finished entering some notes and looked up at Lucas. "The big unanswered question for me is, of course, who killed Chef Truffle? I have my theory, but I need to know if it lines up with your evidence. I can't send off my exclusive story unless I have all the facts."

"Blackhart is a first class criminal, but he is not a murderer. He came pretty close though."

"I'd say so. Trying to persuade Zach and Bradley to jump off a cliff is about as close as you can get to murder."

"I agree, Francie. That's why we questioned him at length. He eventually gave us the information we needed to identify Truffle's killer. It's also part of the reason he's remaining in custody. If it weren't for you and June and your fast thinking, things might have turned out very differently."

Ben had been thoughtfully quiet at first, taking everything in, but as the conversation progressed, the suspense finally got to him. "So tell us already! If it wasn't Blackhart, who killed Truffle? I can't believe it was the cabin boy. He can't be much older than me."

"The cabin boy Levi turned out to be Truffle's half-brother. He's older than he looks. In fact he was four years older than Theo."

"But they don't look anything alike." Beth expressed what we were all thinking.

"You're right. Truffle didn't even know who he was. Levi was born before his mother was married. His father was never in the picture. He made his way through the foster system and found himself on the wrong side of the law too many times. When his mother died, his grandmother contacted him and tried to develop a relationship. She told him stories about his family history and showed him photo albums. He became fixated on the story of his great-grandmother..."

"Hazel Henry!" I couldn't help myself. All the bits and pieces were adding up to a full picture at last.

"Yes, Hazel Henry. Rumor had it she was in possession of some items of great value recovered from the Hotel Victory after the fire, but here's where Liz Fuller's statement helped us solidify the charges."

The pieces were falling into place. "She said Levi told her to get the treasure map from Truffle, but the only maps he had were his tattoos, and the only treasure he had was his family. I saw pictures of his tattoos, and they make it pretty obvious how he felt." Remembering the autopsy photos made me sad and angry that a young man would go to such extreme lengths, and in the end it was all for nothing.

"Hamm, next year can we stay home on our anniversary? We can order take-out and watch NetFlix."

"Whatever makes you happy, Francie." He squeezed my hand again, but this time he didn't let go.

Our waiter rushed to the table, waving his hands like he was swatting away an attacker. "Excuse me, but there's a squawking bird in the lobby that keeps trying to fly in here. I don't know who to call, and it won't go away. Can any of you help me? Please! I hate birds! They freak me out."

Everyone at the table stared at me.

"What? Why does everyone think I have some special bond with that flapping feather duster?"

No one moved. They all stared at me.

"Fine."

I got up and walked toward the doorway. Glancing back at my family and friends, I reluctantly left the dining room, entered the lobby, and gave a half-hearted greeting. "Pretty Boy?"

"Cross my heart. X marks the spot. Cross my heart. X marks the spot."

"Fine. Whatever. I hope you're up to date on your shots."

Don't miss out!

Visit the website below and you can sign up to receive emails whenever Olivia Breen publishes a new book. There's no charge and no obligation.

https://books2read.com/r/B-A-QENN-XMQPB

BOOKS 2 READ

Connecting independent readers to independent writers.

Also by Olivia Breen

Lake Erie Mysteries
Sunny Side Up
Deviled
Scrambled

CPSIA information can be obtained
at www.ICGtesting.com
Printed in the USA
JSHW011154120623
43037JS00003B/74

9 798201 515096